The Forward Book of Poetry

2019

BOOKMARK

LONDON

First published in Great Britain by
Bookmark · 83 Clerkenwell Road · London ECIR 5AR
in association with
Faber & Faber · Bloomsbury House · 74-77 Great Russell Street
London WCIB 3DA

ISBN 978 0 571 34767 4 (paperback)

Printed and bound by CPI Group (UK) · Croydon CRO 4YY

MIX
Paper from
responsible sources
FSC® C020471

A CIP catalogue reference for this book
is available at the British Library.

MWA

The Forward Book of Poetry

We hope you enjoy this book. Please return or renew it by the due date.You can renew it at **www.norfolk.gov.uk/libraries** or by using our free library app. Otherwise you can phone **0344 800 8020** - please have your library card and PIN ready.You can sign up for email reminders too.

5 - 6 - S

This anthology was designed and produced by Bookmark, sponsor of the Prizes. Bookmark is a global content and communications company based in London, Toronto, Montreal, Santiago, Lima, New York, LA, Shanghai and Singapore. Bookmark uses consumer insights to develop compelling content for brands that engages consumers and drives sales. Clients include Patek Philippe, Air Canada, LATAM, Bombardier, Fairmont Hotels & Resorts, Explora, Standard Life, Tesco, American Express Travel, Mercedes-Benz, Christie's, Lindt, the Academy of St Martin in the Fields and StreetSmart. bookmarkcontent.com @bookmarkcontent

To Holly Hopkins

Contents

Highly Commended Poems 2018

Foreword

This anthology is a celebration of the variety and brilliance of contemporary poetry, its contents drawn from hundreds of entries to the 27th Forward Prizes for Poetry. As the chair of a jury that includes four poets – Mimi Khalvati, Niall Campbell, Chris McCabe and Jen Campbell – I found an art form that is flourishing in so many ways that no generalisation can do it justice.

It's an honour to have been a part of the process this year and to find that today's poets are looking fearlessly at such a wide range of subjects: freedom fighting to sexual passion, nature to craft, motherhood to nuclear annihilation.

Our shortlist discussions happened during a sunlit May day in Somerset House, when, aided by the evocative drilling of builders outside our window, we brought our months of private reading into the light and discussed our choices. While some may wish for juicy details of conniving judges, vested interests and dark deeds, there was no factionalism, merely a jury of peers who read widely, think deeply and write thoughtfully.

As we compared our individual longlists – in which we discovered much common ground – it became clear that the excellence of the submissions was such that we could fill our shortlists twice over. In the end, the 15 poets in the running for the three individual awards – the Forward Prize for Best Collection, the Felix Dennis Prize for Best First Collection and the Forward Prize for Best Single Poem – are a true rainbow of voices, writers whose subjects cross countries and centuries, who move between styles and registers, and whose artistic identities reflect the wider world in all its nuanced combinations. What they have in common is finesse: the ability to transmute emotions and intellectual approach into work that feels polished, stylish and natural.

As judges, Mimi, Niall, Chris, Jen and I indulged our abiding love of ink on paper and wallowed delightedly in the boxes of beautifully produced volumes that were sent our way. The Forward Prizes honour the written text, salute the power of the printed word and recognise how rewarding and necessary the act of reading is. There are great riches in that solitary absorption and I find it interesting that although we could all have looked at all the submissions online, few of us did. It seems we still love the materiality of the book itself, appreciate the cover images and the overall design, respond to the simplicity of the paper-printed poem and relish reading something in silence, away from a screen and away from other people. We also appreciate the time and attention publishers put into presenting each volume to readers.

Being a poetry editor isn't about fame and profit (although those are nice, and I do hope the Forward Prizes bring some to the shortlistees); it's truly a labour of love and an act of creative integrity. It's excellent to see the wider publishing industry getting behind poetry once more.

This Forward book proves that the question 'Is poetry dead?' really is dead. The Forward Prizes have been instrumental in bringing this about: I have always looked to their shortlists to point me in the direction of poetry's most exciting voices, but the shortlists are not the whole story. In the second part of this anthology – after the shortlisted poets – we have included writers we wanted to commend and celebrate: individual poets that certain jurors raved about, individual poems that one or more of us couldn't get out of our heads.

Given the wealth of talent on offer, I wonder why so many people reach adulthood with an aversion to poetry? I think it boils down to the way it's taught in schools: long, drowsy afternoons counting syllables in a Ted Hughes poem, then having to write an essay ten times the length of the poem, in which you produce a paragraph each on the use of rhyme, rhythm, metaphor and simile, ultimate message and form. That'll squash any enthusiasm out of you and make you think poetry is hard work with no reward.

What needs to happen after that is not discovery but rediscovery, not learning but remembering that we once used to love this form. Indeed poetry is frequently what we loved first, through nursery rhymes. So often it takes a particular poet or poem, or a chance encounter or experience, to return a reader to poetry. For me it was watching Alice Oswald performing in Bristol: a moment of reconnection, of remembering that poetry is not slow and obscure but direct and clear and bright and powerful. I'm hoping the poems featured in this anthology – those highly commended as well as those shortlisted – will provide readers with many such moments of awakening.

Perhaps 'awakening' is the word to hang on to here, with its connotations of mingled realism and revelation. Ultimately, the reasons poetry has survived so long have less to do with formal distinctions, or with individual cultures and civilisations, than with human nature: it comes from and links to our most fundamental drives and actions. Poetry is connected to song and dance, to elegy, to declarations of lust, to lists and snapshots and vignettes, to steady rumination, to haiku and epic, to pillow talk and nonsense rhymes, to sloganeering exhortations and political manifesto, to humour and hurt, satire and beseeching, to remembrance and sorrow and also to appreciative tribute and loving consideration.

In this Forward anthology we invite you to celebrate a thriving community of poets whose words inspire us to go out into the world, to look closely, think generously and feel deeply – and above all to communicate openly.

Bidisha
June 2018

Preface

When I started the Forward Prizes for Poetry in 1992, I was thinking about the people who would respond to poetry if only they encountered the right lines, in the right way, at the right time. I felt, from my own personal experience as a reader, that a poem is a connection – one which can change the way you see the world. And I suspected, but could not prove, that others felt the same.

These days, after 27 annual Forward books of poetry, 27 award ceremonies, I now know that the connection works both ways. A poem can change its reader, yes, but readers also change what is understood as 'poetry'. They seek lines and images that feel apt, true to the times, and if they can't find them in the ranks of already-written poems, they take action.

The young poet Liz Berry, for example, has spoken of discovering with shock that 'life had been pulled from under my feet and flung to the wind' after the birth of her first child. 'I was kept afloat through that lonely, difficult time by the support of other women. In clinics, playgrounds, church halls and messy living rooms, we shared our lives… But when I looked to poems, the place that had always comforted me, that experience was hard to find. It made me feel very lost,' she said in a recent interview for the Forward Arts Foundation website.

Her response was 'The Republic of Motherhood', on page 42: it was 'the poem I'd needed to read when I was pushing my pram through the sleet that long winter'.

Since its first publication in *Granta*, the poem has travelled, becoming both a reason to get in touch with others, and a generator of new communications. On social media, those who had forgotten the bewilderment that followed the translation of their spiky complex selves into the all-smoothing term 'mother' suddenly recovered something lost. 'I was overwhelmed by how many women wrote to me about the poem, telling me that it spoke to their own experiences, letting me into their most vulnerable days,' Berry continued. 'I was emboldened by their companionship and belief in the power of poems to bear witness.'

Like Berry, all the poets in this volume are readers, listeners, viewers, as well as writers; all have stories to tell of specific voices, particular ways of speaking, that spurred them on. For Abigail Parry, the wake-up call came from Maura Dooley's great poem 'History'. 'You could take it apart, like an engine, and examine every part to see what it was doing; at the same time, it worked a spell, and you can't see the joins in a spell.'

The American phenomenon that is Danez Smith tells of being seized through the screen, when watching *DEF Poetry* on HBO. 'It wasn't until I saw poets performing pieces about things I knew about, and places I had been to or seen on TV, using words that sounded like MY words… I didn't know poetry could be contemporary and urgent to my life until then.' Smith's work now reaches enormous new audiences online: on the day after the poem 'dear white America' featured on America's PBS NewsHour, 300,000 people tuned to YouTube for more of the same.

Were they responding to 'poetry' in the abstract? Would any of them even have recognised themselves in the term 'poetry reader'? No, they were drawn by a sense of recognition, a fresh way of speaking about subjects too often deemed too close to the bone, or maybe just too commonplace, for general discussion.

I hope that you, too, find what you seek somewhere in this anthology of the year's best poems. And if you can't – take heart. Do as poets do: read all you can, mind the gaps left by the unsaid, the unspoken, the unspeakable… and illuminate them with words that sound like yours.

This year's Forward Prizes received the highest number of books on record, 207 volumes were read alongside 188 individual nominated poems. The final selection here grew from many hours of thoughtful attention by our judges. Hearty thanks, then, to writer, critic, broadcaster and filmmaker Bidisha, poets Mimi Khalvati, Chris McCabe, and Niall Campbell, and vlogger, poet and author Jen Campbell. They took on box after box of books with enthusiasm; they embraced their task with care.

Thanks are also due to Casey Jones, Robin Castle, Alex Courtley, Fay Gristwood, Lucy Coles and Simon Hobbs and everyone at our sponsors, Bookmark – the content marketing agency formerly known as Forward Worldwide. Bookmark has supported us from the very start: its unswerving dedication and vision, over the past 27 years, is an example to all in literary sponsorship. As well as supporting the prizes, its staff invest a huge amount of expertise and time in the creation of this book.

We are grateful to Arts Council England, to the estate of the late Felix Dennis – which supports the Felix Dennis Prize for Best First

Collection – and to the Esmée Fairbairn Foundation and the John Ellerman Foundation. Thank you, too, to fellow trustees of the Forward Arts Foundation, namely Martin Thomas, Nigel Bennett, Joanna Mackle, Robyn Marsack, Jacob Sam-La Rose, Giles Spackman and Cynthia Miller; to Ben Anslow, who designed this wonderful cover; to Susannah Herbert, the Foundation's executive director, who continues her unstinting work ensuring these prizes punch far above their weight. The team at FMcM have been terrific in promoting the awards – and these anthologies – to a wide public.

Finally, my thanks to Holly Hopkins, Forward Prizes manager, for her rigour, integrity, generosity and good humour.

William Sieghart
Founder of the Forward Prizes for Poetry
June 2018

Shortlisted Poems
The Forward Prize for Best Collection

Vahni Capildeo

Day, with Hawk

for KM Grant

Here among witch-hazels I miss
the peregrine we met just once.
Like the fire from bare twigs that twists
a floral kiss on winter's neck,
He stunned me so I'm hanging on
to language by its clichés, pushed
to singer-songwrite fingernails
down a tumbling slate precipice.
I would call Him chestnut-stippled,
light on the arm, I want to say,
the non-urgent flexing of chest
muscles making a snow-champion's
balance; and bad old hierarchy
doffs its executioner's garb
to rise with the word, princely. Love,
this is; no poem. What is the term
for the gathering of one falcon?
An embarrassment of poets.
An adoration. An abyss.

Bullshit

How to 'lose' or 'abandon' a word? Put it in jail, throw away the key? Then in every reference book or text block, an opaque rectangle shining where it used to be; a myriad lids to a single oubliette. A fort cut out of yellow, living rock; the particular sightlessness that, with the tide, saturates the underground chamber. This is 'having a concrete imagination'. Not breezeblocks. Wet stuff, instantly; ready to be footprinted.

'Bullshit' is the word I would ease into pasture. One year in an élite institution, my progressive male colleagues kept saying 'Bullshit!' They would get me alone; lean in; ask the really-really-really questions. A little way into my her-answers, they would roar in my face: 'Bullshit!' Eyes pared, jaws gaping, a warlock pack of Jacks of Clubs.

If I seemed quiet, it was because of what I was seeing.

Near my childhood home in a new city, a bull is being led down from the low hills. He walks through the diplomatic area to an empty lot. His haunches a big black valentine, swaying. He dumps as he goes. The asphalt doubly steaming.

A great bull is shitting on my street. Let him have quiet enjoyment.

Toby Martinez de las Rivas

In my kingdom it is winter forever.
The snow falls & there is no time nor day –
no distinction between things, no compare,
no flaw to taint our rudimentary clay.

The falcon has flown away with history,
the bullfinch sheathed in ice & snow, the bare
branch shall never know its May,
nor husband teach the vanity of despair.

At Lullington Church/
To My Daughter

Nothing disturbs its peaceful sleep, no dream
of life, no hope, no falsifying dawn
alleviates the blank space within the frame –
no words to speak, no beauty to adorn.

Until she wakes & finds herself alone,
you are her rock, Lord. Lord, you are stone.
Lully, Lulley, Lully, Lulley.

In the marches of his night

A black tarpaulin like the crumpled wings
of seraphim all fallen in one
corner of the field, the yellow stubble
aglow – the rick is burning again in my dreams.
I wake into darkness, reach for you
& find your shoulder beneath my fingers,
your dependable, deep inhalations
coming & going like a life's dynamic
tread between being born & dying,
between the day our sober lips first touched
& what must come: a slow crucifixion.
We have loved each other – haven't we, you
& I? Through the minor difficulties,
the brittleness of feeling, days of complaint?   *Diptych: Waking at 4 a.m.*
Laughed together, consoled each other,
sat through the night, maintained our privacies?
So why, your hand beneath mine, do I
still glimpse in darkness this dancing light?
Look – there goes G.W weeping in frustration,
& I have come in a borrowed car to see
the disconsolate insurance agent,
the woods in silence, the flames in the trees.
Stars, go out: your blithe little faces
do not fit here – they are nothing beside
the pillar of fire that turns my body
orange & black between the pines that wait
to burn at the field's edge & the western
sky's rhetoric of abandonment.

JO Morgan

extracts from **Assurances**

During the early years of the Cold War my father, in his capacity as an R.A.F. officer, was involved in that aspect of bomber-command which dealt with maintaining the *Airborne Nuclear Deterrent*, as it then was. The following takes what I've gleaned of his role over those years and represents it here as a work of variations and possibilities. The scenario itself may be one of routine and repetition, but what I've chosen to draw from it is the undercurrent of waiting, in the ever-present awareness of what is lost when such a waiting is permitted to play out.

.....

Born from a need...

Born from a need to counteract the threat.
Now that such a threat.
For threats have been made.

Now that the enemy has shown that they.
And in sailing so close.
In having simply sailed.

That they could even consider.
That their so-called threats.
That they might launch, and in so launching.

As such a clear need has arisen.
And in its rising.
In its staying up.

A need to negate, to nullify, to rule out.
By our having in place.
By our simply having.

Because if the enemy did.
If the enemy chose.
If, at some point, at length, the enemy.

Because whatever they might send our way.
It wouldn't take long for it to.
From the precise moment of notification.

It wouldn't be.
It would soon be.
It wouldn't.

Four minutes is all we could really expect as.
That's not sufficient for any.
In four minutes there's not enough.

In such a small window there isn't.
Hardly even to get out of. Let alone.
From that initial alarm. From our hearing.

So any counteracting measure must by needs balance out.
And our own force, already deployed, would.
Each and every, at the merest drop.

[...]

When he wakes...

When he wakes each day he winds his watch.
The notched crown growing stubborn as
the hair-thin spring inside is coiled tight.

A precision piece, special issue for navigators,
chronographic. Its circular motions divided,
subdivided, portioned out on separate dials.

At the back of the briefing room he winds it.
The webbing unbuckled, slipped from his slender wrist.
The bright steel poised between his fingertips.

A five-loop strap in airforce grey, the scratchy nylon
softened up by sweat, by daily grime.
He cleans the casing with a cotton bud.

When there is radio-silence he winds it.
The backward ratchet tick held up to his ear outdoing
the thrum of propellers, the hurricane hiss of the air.

Its sweep-hand zeroed with a double click.
Its distance-measure matched to universal machinations
echoed by its dark insides.

When settling down for bed he winds it,
glimpsing the sharp green glow of its dials
in putting out the light.

Each minute mark, each stuttering hand,
adorned with dabs of luminescent paint.
The stored-up brightnesses of day now softly given back.

Danez Smith

from **summer, somewhere**

somewhere, a sun. below, boys brown
as rye play the dozens & ball, jump

in the air & stay there. boys become new
moons, gum-dark on all sides, beg bruise

-blue water to fly, at least tide, at least
spit back a father or two. i won't get started.

history is what it is. it knows what it did.
bad dog. bad blood. bad day to be a boy

color of a July well spent. but here, not earth
not heaven, we can't recall our white shirts

turned ruby gowns. here, there's no language
for *officer* or *law*, no color to call *white*.

if snow fell, it'd fall black. please, don't call
us dead, call us alive someplace better.

we say our own names when we pray.
we go out for sweets & come back.

   //

this is how we are born: come morning
after we cypher/feast/hoop, we dig

a new one from the ground, take
him out his treebox, shake worms

from his braids. sometimes they'll sing
a trapgod hymn (what a first breath!)

sometimes it's they eyes who lead
scanning for bonefleshed men in blue.

we say *congrats, you're a boy again!*
we give him a durag, a bowl, a second chance.

we send him off to wander for a day
or ever, let him pick his new name.

that boy was Trayvon, now called *RainKing*.
that man Sean named himself *i do, i do*.

O, the imagination of a new reborn boy
but most of us settle on *alive*.

   //

sometimes a boy is born
right out the sky, dropped from

a bridge between starshine & clay.
one boy showed up pulled behind

a truck, a parade for himself
& his wet red train. years ago

we plucked brothers from branches
peeled their naps from bark.

sometimes a boy walks into his room
then walks out into his new world

still clutching wicked metals. some boys
waded here through their own blood.

does it matter how he got here if we're all here
to dance? grab a boy! spin him around!

if he asks for a kiss, kiss him.
if he asks where he is, say *gone*.

    //

dinosaurs in the hood

let's make a movie called *Dinosaurs in the Hood*.
Jurassic Park meets *Friday* meets *The Pursuit of Happyness*.
there should be a scene where a little black boy is playing
with a toy dinosaur on the bus, then looks out the window
& sees the *T. rex*, because there has to be a *T. rex*.

don't let Tarantino direct this. in his version, the boy plays
with a gun, the metaphor: black boys toy with their own lives
the foreshadow to his end, the spitting image of his father.
nah, the kid has a plastic brontosaurus or triceratops
& this is his proof of magic or God or Santa. i want a scene

where a cop car gets pooped on by a pterodactyl, a scene
where the corner store turns into a battleground. don't let
the Wayans brothers in this movie. i don't want any racist shit
about Asian people or overused Latino stereotypes.
this movie is about a neighborhood of royal folks—

children of slaves & immigrants & addicts & exile—saving their
    town
from real ass dinosaurs. i don't want some cheesy, yet progressive
Hmong sexy hot dude hero with a funny, yet strong, commanding
Black girl buddy-cop film. this is not a vehicle for Will Smith
& Sofia Vergara. i want grandmas on the front porch taking out
    raptors

with guns they hid in walls & under mattresses. i want those little
    spitty
screamy dinosaurs. i want Cecily Tyson to make a speech, maybe
    two.
i want Viola Davis to save the city in the last scene with a black
    fist afro pick
through the last dinosaur's long, cold-blood neck. But this can't be
a black movie. this can't be a black movie. this movie can't be
    dismissed

because of its cast or its audience. this movie can't be metaphor
for black people & extinction. This movie can't be about race.
this movie can't be about black pain or cause black pain.
this movie can't be about a long history of having a long history
    with hurt.
this movie can't be about race. nobody can say nigga in this movie

who can't say it to my face in public. no chicken jokes in this movie.
no bullet holes in the heroes. & no one kills the black boy. & no
    one kills
the black boy. & no one kills the black boy. besides, the only reason
i want to make this is for the first scene anyway: little black boy
on the bus with his toy dinosaur, his eyes wide & endless

                    his dreams possible, pulsing, & right there.

Tracy K Smith

New Road Station

History is in a hurry. It moves like a woman
Corralling her children onto a crowded bus.

History spits *Go, go, go*, lurching at the horizon,
Hammering the driver's headrest with her fist.

Nothing else moves. The flies settle in place
Watching with their million eyes, never bored.

The crows strike their bargain with the breeze.
They cluck and caw at the women in their frenzy,

The ones who suck their teeth, whose skirts
Are bathed in mud. But history is not a woman,

And it is not the crowd forming in a square.
It is not the bright swarm of voices chanting *No*

And *Now*, or even the rapt silence of a room
Where a film of history is right now being screened.

Perhaps history is the bus that will only wait so long
Before cranking its engine to barrel down

The road. Maybe it is the voice coming in
Through the radio like a long-distance call.

Or the child in the crook of his mother's arm
Who believes history must sleep inside a tomb,

Or the belly of a bomb.

Annunciation

I feel ashamed, finally,

Of our magnificent paved roads,

Our bridges slung with steel,

Our vivid glass, our tantalizing lights,

Everything enhanced, rehearsed,

A trick. I've turned old. I ache most

To be confronted by the real,

By the cold, the pitiless, the bleak.

By the red fox crossing a field

After snow, by the broad shadow

Scraping past overhead.

My young son, eyes set

At an indeterminate distance,

Ears locked, tuned inward, caught

In some music only he has ever heard.

Not our cars, our electronic haze.

Not the piddling bleats and pings

That cause some hearts to race.

Ashamed. Like a pebble, hard

And small, hoping only to be ground to dust

By something large and strange and cruel.

Shortlisted Poems
The Felix Dennis Prize
for Best First Collection

Kaveh Akbar

Yeki Bood Yeki Nabood

every day someone finds what they need
in someone else
                              you tear into a body
and come out with a fistful of the exact
feathers you were looking for wondering
why anyone would want to swallow
so many perfect feathers
                                        everyone
looks uglier naked or at least
I do my pillar of fuzz my damp
lettuce
                    I hoarded an entire decade
of bliss of brilliant dime-sized raptures
and this is what I have to show
for it a catastrophe of joints this
puddle I'm soaking in which came
from my crotch and never did
dry
          the need
to comfort anyone else to pull
the sickle from their chest seems
unsummonable now as a childhood
pet as Farsi or tears
                                I used to slow
dance with my mother in our living
room spiritless as any prince I felt
the bark of her spine softening I became
an agile brute she became a stuffed
ox I hear this happens
all over the world

Neither Now Nor Never

None of my friends want to talk
about heaven. How there is this eternity
and the one for those
more clerical with their faith
I spend hours each week
saying *I can't hear you*
into a phone and courting the affections
of neighborhood cats, yet
somehow never find time to burn the thigh
of an ox or a stack of twenties. Thought,

penetrate my cloud of unknowing.
I remain a hungry child
and the idea of a land flowing with milk
and honey makes me excited,
but I do wonder what gets left out –
least favorite songs on favorite albums,
an uncle's conquered metastasis,
or the girl whose climaxes gave way to panic,
whose sobs awakened the feeling of prayer in me.
May they be there too, O Lord.
With each second passing over me
may that heaven grow and grow.

Abigail Parry

Girl to Snake

We're not supposed to parley, Ropey Joe.
I'm meant to close my eyes and shut the door.
But you're a slender fellow, Ropey Joe,
                 thin enough
to slip beneath the door and spill your wicked do-si-do
           in curlicues and hoops across the floor.
I'll be here. And I'm all ears –
there are things I want to know.

> *Oh tell me tell me tell me*
> *about absinthe and yahtzee,*
> *and sugarskulls and ginger, and dynamite and hearsay,*
> *and all the girls and boys who lost their way*
> *and the places in the woods we're not to go*
> *and all the games we're not allowed to play –*
> *there are so many things to know.*

My mother's got the supper on the go.
My father will be sagging in his chair.
But you're a speedy fellow, Ropey Joe,
                 quick enough
to slide behind his back, a wicked line of dominoes
           zipping through the hall and up the stairs.
Come on, pal. I'm ready now –
there are things I want to know.

> *Oh tell me tell me tell me*
> *about lightning and furies*
> *and ligatures and diamonds, and zipwires and gooseberries*
> *and all the girls and boys who went astray*
> *and all the ones who never got to go*
> *and all the words we're not supposed to say –*
> *there are so many things to know.*

They told me you were trouble, Ropey Joe.
You've always got to tip the applecart.
But you're a subtle fellow, Ropey Joe,
                    suave enough
to worm your way inside and pin your wicked mistletoe
       above the crooked lintel to my heart.
Come on then, shimmy in –
there are things I want to know.

> *Oh tell me tell me tell me*
> *about hellhounds and rubies*
> *and pretty boys and bad girls, and runaways and lost boys*
> *and all the things that made my mother cry*
> *and all the things he said to make her stay*
> *and all the things we're not allowed to say –*
> *there are so many things to know.*

The Quilt

The quilt's a ragtag syzygy
of everything I've been or done,
a knotted spell in every seam,
the stuff that pricks and pulls. The quilt

began in '96. I scrapped
the blotch batiks and brocatelles
each backward-bending paisley hook
that tied me to my town. The quilt

came with me when I packed and left
– a bad patch, that – you'll see I've sewn
a worried blot of grey and black
to mark a bruisy year. The quilt

advances, in a shock campaign
through block-fluorescent souvenirs
of seedy clubs and bad psytrance
and peters out in blue. The quilt

came with me when I ditched the scene
and dressed myself as someone new
– or someone else, at any rate
and someone better, too – I felt

a charlatan in borrowed suits,
and flower prints, and pastel hues,
but things had turned respectable,
and so I stitched that in. The quilt

has tessellated all of it.
Arranged, like faithful paladins,
are half a dozen bits and scraps
from those who took a turn, then split –

the dapper one, the rugby fan,
the one who liked his gabardine,
the one who didn't want to be   *another patch in your fucking quilt*
but got there all the same. The quilt

is lined with all the bitter stuff
I couldn't swallow at the time –
the lemon-yellow calico
I never wore again. The guilt

snuck into every thread of it
and chafed all through the honeymoon.
I scissored out the heart of it
and stitched it, fixed it, final, here –

with every other bright mistake
I wear, like anyone.

Phoebe Power

Name

my grandmother's name was Chris.
ach ja – Christl.

a chrism, christ with a lemon tongue.
turquoise water inside a glass
wörthersee water
a crystal you take in your pocket or carry
touching your neck

a pair of blue and glass eyes
from a black and white portrait

a ring of yellow hair
Chris
in your army green cap

Christl
a baby lying over a stream
or the picture of a baby

notes on climate change

READING

The more I read on the subject, the more I find I need to know about economics, politics, geography and science. But these are areas I barely studied at school. I am trained to respond to texts: literature, music, the visual arts. Thankfully, I am equipped with the skills to scan and comprehend the main points of articles; this allows me better to understand, but not to do.

BLACKOUT

Coal/oil/gas needs to stay put, in the ground. Reduce emissions to zero.

What if a magician clapped his white-gloved hands and all the machines stopped their cranking and burring, mechanical arms stilled? Stage goes black. Combustion stops.

—

Then chaos; conflict; money wars; people with backyard generators running out to chop wood for fires

—

We could accept the proposition of some of the major religions that the self is nothing. We could let go of the self and allow it to dissolve. With this in mind, changes that are coming are nothing more than a great wave. We wait, death grows towards us and widens its embrace. We don't panic but are still, and it carries us away, at some time or another.

—

But the religions also teach us to save others, before thinking of our own death. Because the world is full of creatures who did not play a part in this.

—

I skip the paragraph on extinction. Yes, so this will happen... 40% of species wiped out (mosquitoes remain, spreading malaria. I hardly ever see them anyway). Birds, a fox sometimes. In the country, sheep. If I want to look at reefs or pangolins I can always stream them.

—

If you're a victim of childhood obesity or an eating disorder, then you will have other things to think about.

—

Fred is thinking about how to make his day in the office stuck to the computer bearable. He's already stopped for lunch and snacked on a couple of Jaffa Cakes. He's meeting Sara after work; he'll also have to find time to pick up supper from the supermarket; for example, a salmon en croûte. He's going to download the game he wants now online while he should be working. If he's got the motivation to-morrow he should get to the gym before work. That'll make him feel good and closer to perfect; at least, closer to ok.

—

Even if your house has been flooded you have other things to con-sider, such as whether you should move, and also, what kind of new kitchen units you and your husband both like.

—

John thinks, when he gets back to England from travelling he'll buy a little second-hand car to run around in. Who are you to say he shouldn't have it?

In general, times when we are able to find happiness correlate with omission of the subject. Most activities function perfectly well without its consideration. Outside work, we can even buy lunch out or a cake and coffee, go out for drinks, purchase a book or record. We can relax in a spa or book a plane ticket to a lesser-known European city, thereby providing a pleasant interruption to the routine and something new to photograph.

—

We can even grow fruit, keep chickens and bees, cook together and have sex. We can wander on mountains, draw or paint the colours and shapes we see around us, sing or join a band. We can learn languages, read about other cultures, or take on Proust. We can learn a skill, like knitting, papermaking or cake decoration. We can go camping, do a cycle trail. We can use the internet to share opinions and keep up to date. We can do this without remembering the subject. We can do most of these things without really thinking.

—

Actually, it crops up. In this part of Austria it crops up whitely, in the absence of snow. A 17-year-old boy told me of his ambition to be a ski instructor. He spends his holidays teaching on the slopes and is paid €200 a day. He loves skiing. But there are fewer and fewer instructors here. This winter was wetter, Christmas was wrong. At the February carnival, one float was painted with unsaid words like the silent victim of a strangling – *Wann wird es wieder richtiges Winter?*

—

In this small town, the elderly walk about over-hot in their antique furs and wool caps pinned with birds' feathers. Maybe a few days a winter, now, can Frau Stellinger put on her best sleek fur to go around town. She takes it off once she's reached the warm bank for her appointment.

On the dry road surface, some triangles of green
bottle glass flash yellow-white with bending rays.
Till rocks melt wi' the sun, my dear,
Till rocks melt.

Shivanee Ramlochan

On the Third Anniversary of the Rape

Don't say Tunapuna Police Station.
Say you found yourself in the cave of a minotaur, not
knowing how you got there, with a lap of red thread.
Don't say forced anal entry.
Say you learned that some flowers bloom and die
at night. Say you remember stamen, filament,
cross-pollination, say that hummingbirds are

vital to the process.

Give the minotaur time to write in the police ledger. Lap
the red thread
around the hummingbird vase.

Don't say I took out the garbage alone and he grabbed me by the
    waist and he was handsome.
            Say Shakespeare. Recite Macbeth for the tropics.
Lady Macbeth was the Queen of Carnival
and she stabbed Banquo with a vagrant's shiv during J'ouvert.
She danced a blood dingolay and gave her husband
    a Dimanche Gras upbraiding.

I am in mud and glitter so far steeped
    that going back is not an option.
Don't say rapist.

Say engineer of aerosol deodorant because pepper spray is illegal,
anything is illegal
Fight back too hard, and it's illegal,
>your nails are illegal

Don't say you have a vagina, say
he stole your insurance policy/ your bank boxes/ your first car
downpayment

Say
he took something he'll be punished for taking,
not something you're punished for holding
like red thread between your thighs.

I See That Lilith Hath Been with Thee Again

Love,
I saw our daughter in the grocery store again.
This time, she'd discarded the old shoes,
because finally,
her hooves are coming through.

She was using her talons to tear through meat packets.

Oh, honey, I frowned.
Your mum is a vegan.
Our daughter followed me to the produce aisle, and she chewed
one carrot, sadly, to try to make me happy. It didn't take.

She could barely tame the wild things of her teeth.

We sat and talked in the trunk of my car for about
fifteen minutes afterwards. I offered to pay for her shopping.
She said,

Mother, don't bother. I'm covered. I've got it
sorted, between the furnace and the fire and
the pit of my stomach does all my flame charring anyway. I'm
set, for days.

She said, "Tell Mum don't worry. I've got a nice place. No boys.
I'm finishing up my degree and I don't dream of having fathers;
not anymore. You raised me well, you can't even tell
where the roots of my hair
used to be."

She said, "I'm sorry I didn't want the same life as you both did."
I guess that's what most mothers want to hear.

Honey, oh honey,
we did good.

Lilith sends us love and photographs of her last kill.
We made a mantelpiece of her baby antlers. We know
how to breathe now, how not to be
ungrateful. We love her; we just
don't want the same things she did.
That's all.

Richard Scott

Dancing Bear

Children bring me coins
to watch him balançoire, tombé –
they imagine he has a
forest inside, they close
their eyes to see him
foraging on a high cliff
above a burnished lake –
belly to the wet earth
but inside is just a savage
who loves with only his
claws, his wild mouth,
tears at honeyed flesh
with his barbed tongue
so I tamed him with
a rod, a crop, my fist –
starved him until he would
dance this way, that way.
At six o'clock you should
see me count my money –
hatfuls of brass and gold.
I uncouple his snout, rub
a drop of lotion in, pour
myself a drink as my
father unzips his bear skin –
places his naked head
on my lap – throat exposed.
He apologises to me
for all the places on my body
his hands have scarred
but I just close his eyes,
sing him to sleep,
nuzzle his ears – a blade
in my other hand.

from **Oh My Soho!**

for Daljit Nagra

All this I swallow, it tastes good, I like it well, it becomes mine...
Walt Whitman

I

Urine-lashed maze of cobble and hay-brick! Oh
chunder-fugged, rosy-lit, cliché-worthy quadrant. I
could not call you beauteous but nightly I've strolled your
Shaftesbury slums for a bout of wink and fumble.

Or hopped the iron-wrought gates of Soho Square, dank-
scented potagerie, to harvest night-blooming buds under ripening
street lamps. Or sloped to the Broadwick bog-house
where the cisterns trickle in harmony like the three-stringed lyre,

where the glory holes flicker pink-tongued. Or jumped the queue for
MANBAR video bar, sweaty fluoro-phoenix risen from the
foundations of MARGARET CLAP'S molly house. All this in lithe
Eros' crosshairs, queer angel atop the meat-rack of

Cleveland Street. Eros wants me cum-crazy, boshed on lust,
but I need a clear head for this trip. I am to be homo-historian –
mean to turn Biogrope to biography, foreskin to forbearer.
    Oh my Soho,
let me linger out tonight. I have rainbow warriors to exhume...

II

So who first kilned the homo holy grail? Was it the hunky
Spartans, those man-on-man love missionaries who queered our
leafy Roman-outpost? Or did changeling Jove himself,
    god-talons
sharp for boy-flesh, his comely-white feathers, fashion our same-

sex revolution? Was Soho still Fleet-pasture then? Ganymede
dozing on his crook, horned goats swelling the coppery paths?
And who might we salute for imported whips, banishment, sober
    castration,
point-and-stare-in-the-marketplace marble-heavy shame?

See, for a man to pierce a man with anything more than just a dick,
    e.g. *AMARE*,
was patheticus. Even Hadrian's bust-worthy boyf, Antinous,
dredged sopping from the Nile, reborn a pink-dwarf constellation,
suffered his queer temples to be sacked and plundered

at the hands of Constantine's Christian gentrification. And didn't
Caesar's bullying become blueprint for our own colonisations?
Filching glittering hoards of conflict minerals, leaving our subjects
    with leather-
bound copies of Leviticus. Centuries of sodomites caged for what?

An aqueduct, Regency marble? And didn't we learn the consul's trick
of bread, circuses, the gruff gladiators' bloodstained six-pack?
Still, what is Rome tonight to the t-shirted ladz bumming menthols
    in the disco line
other than *Caecilius est in horto*? Other than an HBO box set?

III

Silver-crowning Soho, throbbing within the white marble halls
of our British Museum, is the Warren Cup. That
Uranian chalice of Victorian naivety. That blueprint of queer
hope. Smithed when Roman homos would meet in

secret. Unearthed, buffed-up when us homos would still meet in
secret yet worshipped by Warren's velveted posse as a
symbol of freedom and reimagined, fetishised as forward-thinking!
Still there is more to queerness than just trans-historical

bum-fun. More than the cup's glittering nostalgia of myrtle wreath
and leather
strap, of embossed bearded boy-love, of gilded lithe limbs.
What about the modern homosexual's plea for lifestyle, joint-
lodgings, legality? What about love? Oh my Soho, Warren's

cup is no wedding cup but a how-to-fuck cup passed around at toga'd
orgies. A mischievous relic. Every empire, ours included,
has done its savage best to stamp us out, redact our mission – its
violent reception from the permanent collection.

Shortlisted Poems
The Forward Prize for Best Single Poem

Fiona Benson

Ruins

Here's my body
in the bath, all the skin's
inflamed trenches
and lost dominions,

my belly's fallen keystone
its slackened tilt –
for all the Aztec gold
I'd not give up

this room where you slept,
your spine to my right,
your head
stoppered in my pelvis

like a good amen –
amen I say
to my own damn bulk,
my milk-stretched breasts –

amen I say to all of this
if I have you –
your screw-ball smile
at every dawn,

your half-pitched, milk-wild smile
at every waking call,
my loved-beyond-all-reason
darling, dark-eyed girl.

Liz Berry

The Republic of Motherhood

I crossed the border into the Republic of Motherhood
and found it a queendom, a wild queendom.
I handed over my clothes and took its uniform,
its dressing gown and undergarments, a cardigan
soft as a creature, smelling of birth and milk,
and I lay down in Motherhood's bed, the bed I had made
but could not sleep in, for I was called at once to work
in the factory of Motherhood. The owl shift,
the graveyard shift. Feedingcleaninglovingfeeding.
I walked home, heartsore, through pale streets,
the coins of Motherhood singing in my pockets.
Then I soaked my spindled bones
in the chill municipal baths of Motherhood,
watching strands of my hair float from my fingers.
Each day I pushed my pram through freeze and blossom
down the wide boulevards of Motherhood
where poplars bent their branches to stroke my brow.
I stood with my sisters in the queues of Motherhood –
the weighing clinic, the supermarket – waiting
for Motherhood's bureaucracies to open their doors.
As required, I stood beneath the flag of Motherhood
and opened my mouth although I did not know the anthem.
When darkness fell I pushed my pram home again,
and by lamplight wrote urgent letters of complaint
to the Department of Motherhood but received no response.
I grew sick and was healed in the hospitals of Motherhood
with their long-closed isolation wards
and narrow beds watched over by a fat moon.
The doctors were slender and efficient
and when I was well they gave me my pram again
so I could stare at the daffodils in the parks of Motherhood
while winds pierced my breasts like silver arrows.
In snowfall, I haunted Motherhood's cemeteries,

the sweet fallen beneath my feet –
Our Lady of the Birth Trauma, Our Lady of Psychosis.
I wanted to speak to them, tell them I understood,
but the words came out scrambled, so I knelt instead
and prayed in the chapel of Motherhood, prayed
for that whole wild fucking queendom,
its sorrow, its unbearable skinless beauty,
and all the souls that were in it. I prayed and prayed
until my voice was a nightcry
and sunlight pixelated my face like a kaleidoscope.

Sumita Chakraborty

And death demands a labor

When it rains in Boston, from each street rises
the smell of sea. So do the faces of the dead.
For my father, I will someday write:
On this day endeth this man, who did all he could
to craft the most intricate fears, this man
whose waking dreams were of breaking the small bones
in the feet of all the world's birds. Father.
You know the stories. You were raised on them.
To end a world, a god dances. To kill a demon,
a goddess turns into one. Almanacs of annihilation
are chronicled in cosmic time. Go on.
Batter everything of mine that you can find.
Find my roe deer with the single antler. Kill him.
Find a girl, or a woman. Display to me her remains
on some unpaved expanse, like road kill
on Kentucky highways, turning from flesh to a
fine sand made of ground bone, under a sun
whose surface reaches temperatures six times hotter
than the finest crematory. On the surface of the earth,
our remains are in unholy concert with the remains
of all who have gone before and all who will follow,
and with all who live. In this way, our ground
resembles a bone house. Search in my body
for my heart, find it doesn't sit gently
where you learned it to be. Thieve in my armory.
Take my saws, take my torches, and drown
my phalanx of bees. Carve into me the words
of the chronicler of hell. Make your very best
catastrophe. My piano plays loud and fast
although my hands are nowhere to be found.
Father, as you well know, I am but a woman.
I believe in neither gods nor goddesses.
I have left my voice up and down the seam

of this country. I, unlike you, need no saws,
or torches. The bees you drowned will come to me
again. Each time you bear your weapons, I,
no more than a woman, grow a new limb.
Each time you use a weapon, my sinews grow
like vines that devour a maple tree.
When I cry, my face becomes the inescapable sea,
and when you drain blood from a creature,
I drink it. On this day this man died,
having always eaten the good food
amid the angry ghosts, having always made
the most overwrought hells.
On this day the moon waxes gibbous
and the moths breed in the old carpets.
On this day from a slit in the ground rises
a girl who does not live long.
On this day to me a lover turns his back
and will not meet my eye.
On this day the faces of the death-marked
are part-willow, part-lion.
On this day has died an artist of ugly tapestries,
and his wares burst into flame.
On this day endeth this man upon who
I hurl the harvest of this ghostly piano,
and on the surface of this exceptional world
the birds have all come to our thresholds,
our windows and our doors, our floorboards,
our attic crannies and underground storerooms,
wires and railroads, tarmacs, highways,
cliffs and oceans, and have all begun to laugh,
a sound like an orange and glittering fire
that originates from places unseen.

Jorie Graham

Tree

Today on two legs stood and reached to the right spot as I saw it
choosing among the twisting branches and multifaceted changing
    shades,
and greens, and shades of greens, lobed, and lashing sun, the fig
    that seemed to me the
perfect one, the ready one, it is permitted, it is possible, it is

actual. The VR glasses are not needed yet, not for now, no, not
    for this while
longer. And it is warm in my cupped palm. And my fingers close
    round but not too
fast. Somewhere wind like a hammerstroke slows down and
    lengthens
endlessly. Closer-in the bird whose coin-toss on a metal tray never
    stills to one

face. Something is preparing to begin again. It is not us. *Shhh* say
    the spreading sails of
cicadas as the winch of noon takes hold and we are wrapped in day
    and hoisted
up, all the ribs of time showing through in the growing in the
    lengthening
harness of sound – some gnats nearby, a fly where the white
    milk-drop

of the torn stem starts. Dust on the eglantine skin, white powder
    in the confetti of light
all up the branches, truth, sweetness of blood-scent and hauled-in
    light, withers of
the wild carnival of tree shaking once as the fruit is removed from
    its dream. Remain I
think backing away from the trembling into full corrosive sun.
    Momentary blindness

follows. Correction. There are only moments. They hurt.
   Correction. Must I put down
here that this is long ago. That the sky has been invisible for
   years now. That the ash
of our fires has covered the sun. That the fruit is stunted yellow
   mould when it appears
at all and we have no produce to speak of. No longer exists. All
   my attention is

free for you to use. I can cast farther and farther out, before the
   change, a page turned,
we have gone into another story, history floundered or one day
   the birds dis-
appeared. The imagination tried to go here when we asked it to,
   from where I hold the
fruit in my right hand, but it would not go. Where is it now.
   Where is this here where

you and I look up trying to make sense of the normal, turn it to
   life, more life,
disinterred from desire, heaved up onto the dry shore awaiting
   the others who could
not join us in the end. For good. I want to walk to the left around
   this tree I have made
again. I want to sit under it full of secrecy insight immensity
   vigour bursting complexity

swarm. Oh great forwards and backwards. I never felt my face
   change into my new
face. Where am I facing now. Is the question of good still
   stinging the open before us
with its muggy destination pitched into nothingness? Something
   expands in you
where it wrenches-up its bright policing into view – is this good,
   is this the good –

under the celebrating crowd, inside the silences it forces hard
    away all round itself,
where chanting thins, where we win the war again, made thin by
    bravery and belief,
here's a polaroid if you want, here's a souvenir, here now for you
    to watch, unfold, up
close, the fruit is opening, the ribs will widen now, it is all seed,
    reddish foam, history.

Will Harris

SAY

A brick-sized block of grey stone washed ashore on which was carved
the word *SAY*. My dad picked it up at low tide and two months
    later found
another, and another saying *LES*. We worked out that rather than
    a command –
like Rilke's *flow* – it was the name of an old firm, *SAYLES*, which sold
refined sugar, with plantations in the Caribbean and a factory in
    Chiswick.
As capital flows, accumulates and breaks its bounds, so too had
    SAYLES
broken into various subsidiaries. Slipped, dissolved and loosed.
    You find
all kinds of things at low tide. One time, a black retriever came
    wagging up
to me with a jawbone in its mouth. What can't be disposed of
    otherwise –
what can't be broken down – is taken by the river, spat out or lodged

in mud. The SAY brick took pride-of-place on our chest of drawers –
masonry, defaced by time, made part of the furniture. My dad
    decided
to give it to you, in part because you're an artist and he thought it
    looked like
art, but also, which is maybe the same, because it suggested reason
in madness, and made him – made us – less afraid. Last week,
    there was an
acid attack. Two cousins, assumed to be Muslim, having torn off their
clothes, lay naked on the road, calling for help. Passers-by crossed
    the street.
Things break, not flow; it is impossible, however lovely, to see the
    whole

of humanity as a single helix rotating forever in the midst of
     universal time.
Flow, break, flow. That's how things go. Is it? *What are you trying*

to say? After the operation, they stapled shut his stomach. As the scars
healed, it became harder to discuss. He drank as if he had no body
     – nothing
said, admitted to or broken. Flow, break, flow. Gather up the
     fragments.
Now he is back to saying *The country's full. Why are they all men?*
     Four months
ago, in a flimsy hospital gown, the fight had almost left him. In a tone
you'd use to distract a child, the nurse told my mum about her
     holiday to
Sumatra in the early '90s. He likes custard, she replied. We told
     him when
to cough and when to breathe. He clasped a button that controlled
the morphine. Bleep. Bleep. What did the blue and green lines
     mean?
The sudden dips? What was the nurse's name? I chose not to

keep notes. Thoughtful as moss or black coffee, or as the screen of
a dead phone. That's what eyes look like when you really look at
     them.
Inanimate. Moss, though, is alive enough to harvest carbon dioxide,
to grow. Yesterday I googled *thoughtful as moss*, thinking it was from
a Seamus Heaney poem, but only found a description of the poet
"grown long-haired / And thoughtful; a wood-kerne // Escaped
     from
the massacre". At school, we learnt that wood-kernes were armed
peasants who fought against the British in Ireland. I imagined them
(and him) as thoughtful kernels, seeds that had escaped death by
     being
spat out. I am nothing so solid or durable. *What are you trying*

to say? For years I made patterns in the air, not knowing what to say,
then you came and pointed out the paintwork cracked and bubbling
on the wall beside my bed which, though it stank, I hadn't noticed.
The streetlight sparked on beads of damp. Your skin smelt bready,
    warm.
I couldn't say how bare my life had been. The stillness in the room
was like the stillness in the air between the heaves of storm. We
    flowed
into and out of each other, saying – *what?* Saying. Not yet together,
we were incapable of breaking. Cradled in pure being. The paint
    flaked,
exposing streaks of poxy wall. I remembered a church where the
    saints'
faces had been scratched away, taking on a new expression: alien,

afraid. Some days I must look alien to him. Scary. One poet said
the devil was neither *blate nor scaur*, incapable of being scared. I sleep
scared most nights but feel no more holy. Once I pronounced "oven"
often like my mum does, and a friend laughed. The cracks appeared
beneath me. In the years before we met, though I wrote, I was too
    scared –
too scarred – to speak. Flow, flow, flow. I wanted to be carried
    along, not
spat out or upon. That SAY brick picked from the riverbed proved
    that
broken things still flow. *What are you trying to say?* When you asked
me that I closed my laptop, offended. Why? It never mattered what
I said. Whether you speak up or scarcely whisper, you speak with all

you are. To the eye of a being of incomparably longer life – to God
or the devil – the human race would appear as one continuous
    vibration,
in the same way a sparkler twirled at night looks like a circle. In
    darker days

I couldn't say that to my dad, slumped in front of the TV with a mug
of instant coffee. Saying it now only makes me think of times I've
        held
a sparkler – the hiss and flare, the after-smell – which runs counter
to that whole vision. One morning, gagging on his breathing tube,
he started to text my mum, but before he could press send his
        phone
died. He couldn't remember what he tried to say. I can't remember
what I tried to say. Flow, break, flow. You hear me, though?

Highly Commended Poems

Hera Lindsay Bird

Monica

Monica
Monica
Monica
Monica
Monica Geller off popular sitcom F.R.I.E.N.D.S
Is one of the worst characters in the history of television
She makes me want to wash my eyes with hand sanitiser
She makes me want to stand in an abandoned Ukrainian parking lot
And scream her name at a bunch of dead crows
Nobody liked her, except for Chandler
He married her, and that brings me to my second point
What kind of a name for a show was F.R.I.E.N.D.S
When two of them were related
And the rest of them just fucked for ten seasons?
Maybe their fucking was secondary to their friendship
Or they all had enough emotional equilibrium
To be able to maintain a constant state of mutual respect
Despite the fucking
Or conspicuous nonfucking
That was occurring in their lives
But I have to say
It just doesn't seem emotionally realistic
Especially considering that
They were not the most self-aware of people
And to be able to maintain a friendship
Through the various complications of heterosexual monogamy
Is enormously difficult
Especially when you take into consideration
What cunts they all were

I fell in love with a friend once
And we liked to congratulate each other what good friends we were

And how it was great that we could be such good friends,
	and still fuck
Until we stopped fucking
And then we weren't such good friends anymore

I had a dream the other night
About this friend, and how we were walking
Through sunlight, many years ago
Dragged up from the vaults, like old military propaganda
You know the kind; young women leaving a factory
Arm in arm, while their fiancées
Are being handsomely shot to death in Prague
And even though this friend doesn't love me anymore
And I don't love them
At least, not in a romantic sense
The memory of what it had been like not to want
To strap concrete blocks to my head
And drown myself in a public fountain
Rather than spend another day with them not talking to me
Came back, and I remembered the world
For a moment, as it had been
When we had just met, and love seemed possible
And neither of us resented the other one
And it made me sad
Not just because things ended badly
But more broadly
Because my sadness had less to do with the emotional specifics
	of that situation
And more to do with the transitory nature of romantic love
Which is becoming relevant to me once again
Because I just met someone new
And this dream reminded me
That, although I believe that there are ways that love can endure
It's just that statistically, or
Based on personal experience
It's unlikely that things are going to go well for long

There is such a narrow window
For happiness in this life
And if the past is anything to go by
Everything is about to go slowly but inevitably wrong
In a non-confrontational but ultimately disappointing way

Monica
Monica
Monica
Monica
Monica Geller from popular sitcom F.R.I.E.N.D.S
Was the favourite character of the Uber driver
Who drove me home the other day
And is the main reason for this poem
Because I remember thinking Monica???
Maybe he doesn't remember who she is
Because when I asked him specifically
Which character he liked best off F.R.I.E.N.D.S
He said 'the woman'
And when I listed their names for him
Phoebe, Rachel and Monica
He said Monica
But he said it with a kind of question mark at the end
Like...............Monica?
Which led me to believe
Either, he was ashamed of liking her
Or he didn't know who he was talking about
And had got her confused with one of the other
Less objectively terrible characters.
I think the driver meant to say Phoebe
Because Phoebe is everyone's favourite
She once stabbed a police officer
She once gave birth to her brother's triplets
She doesn't give a shit what anyone thinks about her
Monica gives a shit what everyone thinks about her
Monica's parents didn't treat her very well

And that's probably where a lot of her underlying insecurities
    come from
That have since manifested themselves in controlling
And manipulative behaviour
It's not that I think Monica is unredeemable
I can recognise that her personality has been shaped
By a desire to succeed
And that even when she did succeed, it was never enough
Particularly for her mother, who made her feel like her dreams
    were stupid
And a waste of time
And that kind of constant belittlement can do terrible things to a
    person
So maybe, getting really upset when people don't use coasters
Is an understandable, or at least comparatively sane response
To the psychic baggage
Of your parents never having believed in you
Often I look at the world
And I am dumbfounded that anyone can function at all
Given the kinds of violence that
So many people have inherited from the past
But that's still no excuse to throw
A dinner plate at your friends, during a quiet game of Pictionary
And even if that was an isolated incident
And she was able to move on from it
It still doesn't make me want to watch her on TV
I am falling in love and I don't know what to do about it
Throw me in a haunted wheelbarrow and set me on fire
And don't even get me started on Ross

Sean Borodale

Eastwater Cavern Voice-Test

It is almost a passion, the gloom;
bodies, only extravagances of air,
so still, leeched-out
and rich with slumber.

It is almost a mineral, the waste;
gothic, deep and dreadful –
there, that appointed word
which corners the voice:
Dread.

Almost a snuff, the red paste earth,
almost acoustic
pressing the voice back into the blackness of the throat;

muffling, before it steadies;
absorbed
into dry, scaly galleries of rock;
ruptured, torn into deeper fathoms.

Terms such as 'bedding plane'
do nothing to obscure the illness of the place.

A rough, dry decline;
so thin after that, so weak and variable.

The only route: to drop deeper, irreversible.
Lie at a gruesome end
as a heap in a heap,
the instrument of the bones.

So strangely wooden;
so curled and dismantled. Shrunken;

something a pilgrim would smooth with his feet.

Graham Burchell

Resurrection

I know they ashed my flesh, milled my bones,
sealed the flour of my body in a casket,
and buried it out of sight on the north side
of the churchyard, to be half sunk flotsam,
caught in a wave of tombstone buoys whose tip
and sway through the calm between tempests,
cannot be measured by those who disposed me
to memory.

I know it was October. I was ashed but still here.
On a moonlit night I crawled out
feeling damp turf against toes, knees and palms
that I no longer owned. I sensed without discomfort,
a chill washing over skin no longer worn.
Tongueless, I tasted the air, the turn of leaves
about to drop.

I know I was not alone. Others came out of the earth,
looked skyward. There was light, birdsong, voices.
One brushed dirt from clothes with fingers
long since whispered to dust.
Here stood the assured and the confused, leaning
on lichen-crusted markers of their mortal lives.

I know one had his old moon face buried into folded arms.
Others, dressed in the way of their day, greeted
like old pals across the gap; a spark
between their eternal bed and the next.
Many, like me were naked.
Perhaps we were the burned ones;
alternative members of the same occasional club.

I know a young man in a white collarless shirt,
reached out a hand that was once his own.
His other pointed to stone-carved words;
Charlie, who fell asleep in nineteen nineteen,
in his seventeenth year. He blinked, not at my nakedness.
We didn't care. And I know in a far away voice
he said, *I believe this is your first?*

Marianne Burton

For A Long Time He Was Very Childish

School Evaluation for Søren Aabye Kierkegaard

For a long time he was very childish,
the most provoking and the least serious.

His small stature and death of a brother
may have caused some wariness of others,
but he is unspoilt, clever, merry and open,
and thoroughly versed in his religion.

Love of freedom and an occasionally amusing lack
of restraint prevents him embracing any topic
too deeply; he seems afraid if he commits it might
be difficult to pull back. But this tendency should abate.

There has been notable progress in the last year
and when the university allows his intellect to prosper
he will surely be counted a most able scholar
and come to resemble his elder brother.

Toby Campion

When the Stranger Called Me a Faggot

I did not blink

instead   this time   my mouth filled with
Grimsby's chip cone, wooden forks
and Aylestone Leisure Centre, rolling hills, walks to school,
my first cigarette bought off Josh Baker for 50p
and the taste of being short-changed and the taste of being told
it is fair, K-Swiss, The Old Horse, my overworked father,
uncles asking about girlfriends at Christmas, my cousin's knee,
my broken nose and the kitchen roll unable to soak up
a family's damage, funeral faces, graffiti
on the back of our livers and Churchgate, Maryland Chicken,
free entry before eleven, bottles tossed into dancing crowds,
lips greeting glass with crimson splutterings of *hallelujah*,
and fifth period French, savages born of boredom,
fighting Ashley down the science block, crowd of camera-phones
blocking us in, no way out for one
and Nickesh and Chris and Sam,
Mecca Bingo and wash brook, the boy who got snatched,
chewing gum sticking eyelashes together,
football practice and get it together lads,
my hand on his leg, shower room and eyes forward lads,
his hand in my mouth
and or what or what or what.

and my new friends said,
we haven't heard you like that before

and I said,
you haven't heard me.

JR Carpenter

from **Notes on the Voyage of Owl and Girl**

// The Voyage.

An owl and a girl most ['adventurous', 'curious', 'studious'] ['set out', 'set sail', 'sailed away'] in a ['bottle-green', 'beetle-green', 'pea-green'] ['boat', 'sieve', 'skiff', 'vessel']; a ['beautiful', 'shipshape', 'sea worthy'] ['craft', 'raft', 'wooden shoe'], certainly, though a ['good deal', 'wee bit', 'tad'] too ['small', 'high in the stern'] to suit the two of them. They took a ['bushel', 'barrel', 'bundle'] of ['honey', 'money'] and an ['almanac', 'astrolabe', 'barometer', 'chronometer'] of dubious ['accuracy', 'origin', 'usefulness']. The owl was ['actually', 'basically', 'simply', 'slightly'] ['home sick', 'sea sick', 'sceptical', 'terrible with directions', 'a nervous traveller']. The girl sought to gain ['definitive', 'further', 'first-hand'] ['knowledge', 'experience', 'proof'] of ['the Northwest Passage', 'Ultima Thule', 'a strange phenomena known as sea lung'].

According to my ['calculations', 'library books', 'test results'], the girl informed the owl, it's ['six', 'seventeen', 'twenty-seven'] ['leagues', 'knots', 'nights', 'nautical miles'] ['due north', 'north', 'northeast'] of here. Her ['mother', 'great-aunt', 'grandmother'] had been among the most revered of ['authors', 'experts', 'philosophers'] on this topic. But the girl had her own ['life to live', 'line of inquiry', 'ideas', 'theories'].

The owl said, ['Birds of a feather stick together', 'Loose lips sink ships', 'Everywhere we go, there we are'].

How soon he ['drifted', 'floated', 'sailed', 'veered'] off ['topic', 'course', 'track', 'radar']!

According to my ['spyglass', 'sea chart', 'sextant', 'sonar'], we're nearing the edge of ['our story', 'our journey', 'the earth', 'this narrow sea'], the girl said, but still they sailed ['for a year and a day', 'on through the night', 'on until well past bed time'], ['despite the wet and sea fret', 'by the light of the silvery moon', 'across the North Atlantic', 'on a river of crystal light', 'into a sea of dew'].

By this time, all the owl's ['magazine subscriptions', 'snack food items', 'phone card credits', 'batteries'] had run out.

Don't ['fret', 'jinx us', 'obsess', 'second-guess'], said the girl most ['ardently', 'rationally', 'seriously']. The ['diaries', 'letters', 'lists', 'ships' logs'] she kept constitute the entirety of the ['knowledge', 'evidence', 'proof', 'records', 'traces'] we have left of this ['impossible', 'implausible', 'improbable'] voyage toward ['the edge of the earth', 'the fountain of youth'].

Sophie Collins

Healers

I encountered a scaffold
outside the Holy Trinity Church in Vladimir.
At first I didn't notice her
slumped against the side of the church –
she was pretty small for a scaffold, pretty un-
assuming. Her safety mesh
was torn in places and sun-bleached all over
and threatened to dislodge
due to a forceful wind that was typical
of the season. She was shaking.
She was fundamentally insecure.
She told me that good foundations are essential
but the men who had put her together
hadn't taken advantage of the right opportunities.
Now, each day, someone came by
called her 'unsafe' and also 'a liability'
then left, failing to initiate the dismantling process
that yes would have been painful
and slow, but kinder.
International visitors to the church
blamed her for the mess of tools and rags
on the grounds and for the fact
that they could no longer see
the church's celebrated mural
depicting Saint Artemy of Verkola
unusually pious
highly venerated
child saint killed by lightning.
His dead body radiated light
never showed signs of decay
and was in fact said to have effected
multiple miracles of healing.
I said comforting things to the scaffold

but she only seemed to lean more heavily
against the side of the church.
We are rarely independent structures she said
before she dropped a bolt pin
which released a long section of tube
which released another bolt pin
which released several wooden boards
which scraped another tube
and made an unbearable sound.

Sarah Corbett

The Unicorn

after Rilke

It wasn't there, and yet we believed in it,
the milk-white beast, barleycorn twist of its
impossible horn, horn now proven
to be narwhal tusk; oh how we love proof.

It wove itself into the tapestry
of myth where we chained it in gold filigree;
let's say, yes, it is gold that enslaves it.
Its chaste self saves us if we imagine it.

In the garden where the pomegranate
evolves its own bloody secret
the creature that has never been
tentatively puts out one silver hoof,

shimmering and oblique as an antique
mirror into which we can no longer see.

Emily Critchley

Something wonderful has happened it is called you

And mostly these days I just like to look
at you and sometimes make words
out of your name or rock you
in my arms till the thought of I
with or without poetry
no longer matters.
It's not like I have forgotten
how to worry

   – the disappearing forests
     vanishing species
     zone of sky above our heads –

I pray that when you are older there may still be
the forests, for instance, and the species

   – precious zone of sky
     to keep sun off yr precious face –

And not just in the zoo.
I worry about other things too but mostly
it is hard to be unhappy these days
especially now the spring's advancing
and you're learning
about hands, how to hold things in them
and take everything it's yours.

Paul Deaton

That Bang

I curl in bed like an ammonite,
thinking what valleys my ribs will leave
in the mattress soft sediment.

The exposed contours of bones
linked like the constellations of stars.
Here lies my foot,

the half-moon bay of my hunter's heel.
My skull a deflated football,
thin as bird-broken eggshell.

I wish to descend,
see life in the era of ferns,
pre-school, pre-man.

Yet time is travelling the wrong way.
Some say it is speeding up.
Those from Cambridge;

physics and the universe's tidal outwash flow.
That Big Bang.
Louder than an Alpine thunderclap.

I hold the space between stars.
The hour's no-hour.
And, as in alleyways, I hold too, the concentrated blackness.

Christopher Deweese

I was a wartime censor

I was a wartime censor
seeding letters with sudden shadows
like visual static,

a hundred possible sentences
aging the vague, contagious darkness.

Where there had been cities,
I left islands.

I worked in complete silence.
Our blockade's machinery
had been undertaken
on a scale so unprecedented

that curtains of fog
surrounded my desk

as if mirroring the distant, storm-beaten ships
I kept trying to protect.

A quiet jubilation
consumed my rejoicing hands
in something like affection

whenever I found a metaphor
overlooked by my platoon.

Chess moves to coordinates off the table.
Postcards that read only
I believe you owe me a letter.

Imtiaz Dharker

Wolf, Words

In another room, the children are pigs.
You can hear them truffling behind sofas,
bumping chairs, snuffling round table-legs.

From the dregs of a story, the wolf
inks in, pulled to the sound of breathing,
drawn to the warm, the living,

rasping, *Let me in. Let me in.*
In their literal world, the children believe
the wolf is a wolf not a wolf made of words.

They make themselves small behind closed doors
in a house made of straw and a house made of sticks
and a house made of bricks, in a time

made of tricks. But the breath of the wolf
is the breath of the world. It blows a flurry
of straw, a volley of twigs, a fall

of rubble down on the pigs
who come squealing, squalling out of the storm
to a house made of words. This.

Scratching at walls, something is out there,
ever and after, something that howls.
What outcast word, what unhoused soul?

Tishani Doshi

Girls Are Coming Out of the Woods

for Monika

Girls are coming out of the woods,
wrapped in cloaks and hoods,
carrying iron bars and candles
and a multitude of scars, collected
on acres of premature grass and city
buses, in temples and bars. Girls
are coming out of the woods
with panties tied around their lips,
making such a noise, it's impossible
to hear. Is the world speaking too?
Is it really asking, *What does it mean
to give someone a proper resting?* Girls are
coming out of the woods, lifting
their broken legs high, leaking secrets
from unfastened thighs, all the lies
whispered by strangers and swimming
coaches, and uncles, especially uncles,
who said spreading would be light
and easy, who put bullets in their chests
and fed their pretty faces to fire,
who sucked the mud clean

       off their ribs, and decorated
their coffins with briar. Girls are coming
out of the woods, clearing the ground
to scatter their stories. Even those girls
found naked in ditches and wells,
those forgotten in neglected attics,
and buried in river beds like sediments
from a different century. They've crawled
their way out from behind curtains
of childhood, the silver-pink weight

of their bodies pushing against water,
against the sad, feathered tarnish
of remembrance. Girls are coming out
of the woods the way birds arrive
at morning windows – pecking
and humming, until all you can hear
is the smash of their minuscule hearts
against glass, the bright desperation
of sound – bashing, disappearing.
Girls are coming out of the woods.
They're coming. They're coming.

Sarah Doyle

The woman who married an alchemist

He chose me for my dullness, he told me; the challenge
of it, of replacing my sickly patina with glow. I know
a project when I see one, he said, appraising the weight
on me, the soft lead bulk that settled round my bones.
He set to work, stoking fires and sweltering at phials,

pinching my skin between his thumb and forefinger,
a fever of text coiling from his lips. He stroked
my breasts, my belly, my hips with a practised hand,
though never with a man's desire; I was metallurgy,
and no match for his iron resolve. Those first weeks,

my blood fizzed with heat and my pores secreted a
sulphurous odour whose rotting breath choked the air
around me. He was mercurial: shrill with triumph
at every slight yellowing, bitter with recriminations
when the grey of my tarnish bloomed once more.

He dowsed me with water, kindled flames at my feet,
packed me in salt. It was my fault, I was never more
than alloy, a bastard mix that was temporary at best.
He radiated ire, raged that I had the brass neck to stand
there, useless as pyrite, fool that I was. He considered

veneering my skin with gilt, but would always feel
the difference, he said; how my lustre was superficial,
lacking the subcutaneous value he craved. I willed
myself to shine for him, but was made of baser stuff.
Never golden. Never precious. Never good enough.

Sasha Dugdale

For Edward Thomas

Not a cloud in the sky and the pier hangs in mist
No swiftness and not a cloud to mark this soul
But brightness all around so fiercely torpid
Nothing can be seen at all.

The front is so wide I walk with my eyes closed
And the sea breathes shallow as a roosting dove
My unblemished soul goes shapeless through the light:
Pale calf-hide, it has need of the cloud's love.

There you stand, like the fish upon its tail,
Who tasted all the various hells upon the earth
And was marked for ever by the passage of a cloud
And the rain, and the birds, and all such things of worth.

Kate Edwards

Frequency Violet

Some have misgivings about Violet. They believe
she is on the spectrum; somewhere at the very end,
in fact. None can account for it but we're told
she hums inaudibly in the octave of ozone, and lives
in an airlock, loiters in restricted zones, makes
uncanny utterances, keeps marine snails, crushes
pencils into graphite dust, dances like it's the seventies,
tattoos the world's conspiracy theories onto uterine vellum,
stays up all night smoothing polymers under strip lights,
blinking. Rumours insist she has an eye for tactical missile
design and stockpiles blueprints, knows how to execute
the perfect gem heist and leave fingerprints all over it.
Her party trick will make volatile hearts and auras
of loneliness glow in the dark; despondency shine black.
Dreams of Violet often precede a wedding or a gas attack.

Richard Georges

Now / Tortola

you lie beneath my tongue
shivering your last restraints into the wave

I drink happily

you ripen like fruit in my mouth
your eyes slitting the darkness open

& we are one with it

Lucy Hamilton

Blood Letting

I

The Engineer says the priest came to hear her confession but she couldn't think of anything terrible she'd done. [The dialyzer is the key to haemodialysis.] She is tearful & apologetic. Calls herself *grouchy mess* & *hysterical witch*. She's so wired-up that the 'ports' look like multi-coloured hair bobbins. [The average person has 10 to 12 pints of blood; during dialysis only one pint (about two cups) is outside the body at a time.] I collect up phone, cards & photo of L. Follow her bed out of the HDU back to the ICU. Sometimes her large brown eyes seem to rest on me.

II

Sometimes her brown eyes settle on me. Like a butterfly on my skin. Her hair is feather-soft. She complains it hasn't been washed. [There are two sections in the dialyzer; the section for dialysate and the section for blood.] The nutritionist asks what she likes to eat. *Anything Mediterranean*. Then removes the untouched sausage & mash. [The two sections are divided by a semi-permeable membrane so they don't mix together.] I hold the Engineer's hand. We look at the photo of L. Fifteen & sitting her mocks.

III

Other times her eyes are eloquent. Large white rather than brimstone yellow. The nurse explains why she keeps being moved between IC & HD. Her washed hair fans out dark against the pillow. [The dialysis solution is then flushed down the drain along with the waste.] We talk about medieval blood letting – she almost laughs. Doctors optimistic but. Stress situation might change & suddenly.

IV

Nor butterfly nor Engineer. Eyes barely slits in *setae*. No more to flit from iPhone to photo. Never to rest on me. Nor blood nor dialysate – the machines are silent, pushed aside. Her head seems slighter, hair curtained against her face, lips a little parted. One cold hand grips an olive wood cross. As I lean to kiss her brow, it's as if she chose to speak ... *For, if I imp my wing on thine, affliction shall advance the flight in me.*

Philip Hancock

The Girl from the Triangle House

for Kerry Davis

A gunshot in a one-horse town
is the clack of the latch
of her garden gate. Starlings flit
to the pylons. Boundary hawthorns stir.
Our trailing feet brake the roundabout.

Lithe and angular with a paprika Afro,
she jigs behind a World Cup football.
Forty keep-ups then shooting-in;
Rigger's drawn the short straw,
paddles in the crater beneath the crossbar,

always fooled by her touch.
The ball gummed to the criss-cross
lacing of her left boot, I'm wrong-
footed by her step-over,
undone by her nutmeg.

Simple passing long after the Evening Sentinels
have been posted and the three blind mice run off
with Giannasi's Ices, until paraffin heat
sweats greenhouse panes and empty buses
flicker between the houses like cine film.

Tonight, the stone I dribble along the pavement
won't escape me. I turn for home,
head full of those orange freckles
coming out like stars, of boots like hers,
Pumas with the white flash.

Emily Hasler

The Built Environment

a waste and ownerless place
　　　　Botolph

There is in this place as little as can be
imagined, so things stand in for each other:
metal turns to wood, wood
to bone, ruins to wrack—
in this already regretting wind,
both scourge and the salt to heal it.

The air is most of the materials
needed for the church and the best
of the gutting fire. This creamy crag
is a flushwork of creatures, late of the land.
Moving mudstone is a tracery of bubbles
forming, bursting, flat and still as water,
thick and permanent as the first render—
a thin layer that dries as it cracks.

Ellen Hinsey

Evidence THE LAWS

ARTICLE 1.

It is forthwith declared: if by the homeland of their ancestors they are *strangers*—so shall their children be *strangers* too—

ARTICLE 2.

If so identified as *strangers*—they shall no longer be fit to dwell under the common, rough-timbered sky—

ARTICLE 3.

If they labour in the cities, they shall no longer reside in the cities; if they live in the country, they shall be deprived of even the wind-scattered sheaves—

ARTICLE 4.

If thus, they find themselves without labour: *their idleness shall be punishable;*

ARTICLE 5.

And, if the Laws have once pronounced judgment upon them: they shall be forbidden speech in the crowded market square—

ARTICLE 6.

If they find themselves without land, wealth or voice: the *stranger* shall live within the tight confines of the journey—

ARTICLE 7.

Where hours shall be their daily bread and rustic nightfall their only shelter—

And if, by chance or destiny, a *stranger* should love a *non-stranger*, they too shall be punished—

ARTICLE 9.

Nor shall they benefit from counsel in the white interrogation rooms.

ARTICLE 10.

Where iron hooks shall be roughly affixed to pillars in Justice's basement.

ARTICLE 11.

And although those in attendance shall bear false witness, they will be exempt from forty stripes—

ARTICLE 12.

For no one shall preside over the Laws: *for my beloved, have no doubt—we too are the generation of the Flood.*

Lindsey Holland

Confession of a Need to Know

I dream that crows are detectives whose job
is to pick through evidence—carrion, bone, alibi—

and shield us from *murder* (they've been maligned
by that collective noun). It's why they loiter

at junctions and laybys, feign a casual jaunt
in stubble fields and lope along stone walls.

I want to be a crow and you don't. I hope
this won't be a problem.

I dream of cut-out crows at sundown
in ritual dance. *Chatterings* of choughs

on crags, braced against rain. *Clatterings*
of jackdaws like automatons. Conjugal crows

in derelict towers. A nauseous sensation
on a train, two hundred miles an hour

to crow-eyed stillness. They keep bad *tidings*
(a good one, that) to their chests. The noble crow,

mission held in its cloak. I watch one bird,
whiskered beak jagging in a hole, unearth

a gunmetal box, crushed up, a magazine
that's spent its bullets. Others *congregate*

(a helpful noun, for the magpie), peering
from a backdrop of fog, their blackness

hugged by ghosts. They ponder, never quite
harnessing judgement. Not villains

but sentries, observers who caw in both alarm
and tenderness. Crows who slip

through time, appearing at waysides
with heads atilt, doffing unseen caps.

Crows who aren't mafia but keep a tally
of the bodies. I'm sorry

that I overlooked, misconceived,
but we've all done the same. 'A carrion crow

sat on an oak' the nursery song goes,
and it taunted, but crows don't taunt, we only

imagine that they do. Crows pluck at fact
and leave a skeleton. Protectors on the rim

of something pale and rotten. True crows.
Crows who snib-up intelligence. Maybe

I once knew their world but have forgotten.
I want to know. I hope this won't be a problem.

Ian Humphreys

Return of the Discotheque Dancers

   Come back, come back – you glistening boys,
you clerks and scholars, farmhands, plumbers,
   you make-up artists, money men, you lives

hacked short. You oh-so-very-dazzling, you boho
   fops, you preachers, poachers, lovers, sons. My sons.
Years ago we buried you in shame. You bore the guilt

   as night closed in. *So Many Men, So Little Time*,
the chorus rang. When the dry ice lifted
   and the spotlight glowered, so many friends were gone.

Rise up! Break free of soil, of stone, of ivy's snare.
   Come chase the hare, the handsome fox. Rattle cages,
shake your bones, come back for one last wicked

   whirligig. Imbibe the city – its bars and clubs,
its tribes and scars. Refrains that moved us then will tug
   the moon. Shed your shirts, your wounded skin,

shatter the glass dance-floor. Our song's half-sung
   so flex your voices, roar like guns. Tallulah's waiting!
Devilish nuns are roller-skating!

   Come back, come back – you glistening boys.
Let's march again at *Bang, Scandals, Napoleons,*
   Spats, Subway, Copa's and Heaven, Heaven, Heaven!

Ishion Hutchinson

A Burnt Ship

Tiger moth, hair smoke, silk tied,
her mouth's not the chamber angel,

the night chimera that comes
to the boy on the alabaster throne,

no longer child-king of Sumer,
his trigger-blood hammers rust,

strings of charm, shards of jewels
glint like sunset oil, streak shield

held closely in the singing woods
of bat-eaten fruits, silently hanging

blot seeds, cut sage and rosemary,
a blight mercury, cured meat,

silver streams dividing undersea
the ultraviolet weeds, plankton,

seahorse, half man, sunken masks,
god's horn, perfume, ivory tusks,

market dust, vine pillars, batter-ram
sound, orange-light caravan, wheels

of water spinning industry, whipped
backs, shock foil, the galvanised wax

congealed dreams of a burnt ship;
all were lost, all were drowned.

Jackie Kay

Vault

(after Marion Coutts, For the Fallen)

And just when we thought, when we thought, when we thought
         We could not   we could not
        We did, we did   we leapt, we leapt
        We made it   across, across.
       We fell often   were broken; we lost.
      The past is a leap   in the dark: a dark horse.
          We laughed. We wept. Of course, of course.

Amy Key

Haunted

The little girl who died after eating buttercups is haunted. The Gold Lion and the two Red Lions are haunted. Following the death of a dog, the driver of a car and its two passengers, the zebra crossing at the infant school is haunted. The old wooden bus shelter near the gated park is rumoured to be haunted. Under the pier, at the high tide mark, is haunted. The dog known as 'Handsome' haunts the perimeter of the library. The butcher's father, Ted the elder, forbade the making of beef sausages following the death of a customer in 1973, who subsequently haunts the butcher's. Discarded peanut shells under cinema seats are haunted. The Liberal Club is haunted by a cat named 'Jinx' who will drink shandy, but only from an ashtray. Penelope Caldwell, daughter of the last Town Crier, haunts the civic centre. The last Town Crier haunts the derelict toilet block of the private Boys' School. Persons unknown haunt the 377 bus route. The defunct ticket machine in the delicatessen is haunted. Constance Bown, lifetime companion of Penelope Caldwell, haunts the duck pond. The entire contents of the laboratory, including the Bunsen burners, pipettes, volumetric flasks, tongs, microspatulas, goggles, beakers, crucibles and magnesium strips, are haunted. The trees by the new roundabout are haunted, though they've mostly been cut down.

If you have the urge to swallow pebbles, it is a ghost.
If you wake up with your hair all about the pillow as though you arranged it for photographic reasons, it is probably a ghost.
If when you close your eyes you can remember your first taste of butter, it is a ghost.
If your cat paws the place you were sitting when you leave the room, your cat is a ghost.
If you lie in bed emphatically alone, you are a ghostly presence.
If you can't see a ghost but can see yourself very small, it is most definitely a ghost.

John Kinsella

Sweeney Dreams He's having a Nightmare of Clearing

In his dream Sweeney sees himself de-feathered and crashed in the
  grey sand,
unable to pull himself out of sleep, locked into a nightmare of a
  bulldozer
running across the land like an electric razor, the entire bush falling
to its gigantic all-encompassing blade. Nothing stops it, not even
the largest jarrah and marri trees, nothing just nothing will thwart
its progress, not even boulders setting their shoulders against
the onslaught. Sweeney in his dream tries to stop the nightmare
in its tracks, and calls on those who have become his friends to
  help him:
Forgive me for my mis-sayings for my well-meant efforts that have
  failed.
Forgive me for not spreading my wings wide enough to protect
  you all.
And with that he rises from the sand and squawks so loud the driver
halts his deadly machine, and leaps down and jabs his finger
into Sweeney's charred breast, like an image out of a painting
yet to be painted, and says, Now listen, buster, this is how I make
my living, and who are you to take food from my table?! And
  Sweeney,
feeling the sway of his argument and feeling himself fall back
into the nightmare, sees his own beak moving, hears his own words
tumble past the nub of his tongue in more than mimicry of a
  human voice:
But when it's all gone, you'll have no more work anyway and the
  world
will be dying. And the bulldozer driver replies, You may be right,
but what would you have me do? – this is my job, and I know no
  other.
And with this Sweeney wakes, from both dream and nightmare
  and sweating

and feeling for his feathers to find them black and red and white
   and intact,
and says: I will fly high and watch over them all, I will fly from
   grey sand
over gravel and ochre loam and granite and brown clay. And in
   doing so
he flies past Walwalinj which the colonisers call Mount Bakewell,
and watches the fires the farmers have lit to eat their stubble and
   chaff
from the last harvest running over their firebreaks into the shreds
   of bush
remaining from past clearings and past *burnings-off*, and he watches
   a digger
knocking down four magnificent York gums – ancient solar systems
of life – to make a paddock even more vacant, more productive
in the short term, but dead to the future, and he cries and cries
but his tears put out neither the fires nor the work-zeal of the clearer
doing a job as night falls, and the kangaroo's head is renamed
the Southern Cross and the ends of the earth play
on the stereos of machinery and cars and houses
and personal devices. Sweeney
in his dream of a nightmare.

Anna Kisby

Sea Lily

My eldest daughter, sixteen this week, is hollering
from the tub for a towel. From her window
she sees all the way to the coast – we are close
but we do not flood.

On Jupiter's moon, Europa, there is a sea
where underwater lilies wait for discovery.
Free-swimming larvae grow into juveniles
fixed to the ocean floor by a stalk.

Sea lilies have ten arms waving. Nerves.
A mouth that sings, at some alien frequency.
They are lit from within. They are their own
most important thing.

I haven't been in for a while. She is overspilling
the bath. When she reaches out through petals
and bomb-glitter I see her armpit hair is long,
dyed sea-foam green.

Vanessa Kisuule

an introduction to sorcery

i often dream of sorceress women
illuminated by restless firelight
all wearing different versions of my face

these crazy bitches squabble
over everything and nothing
they hold the blunt edge of the past
to each other's necks – threaten to slice

it is nothing less than
inevitable to watch them
split open like coconuts
an oddly tender excavation

examining all their fingers in turn
i do not even flinch at the blood, gristle
and ink cocktailing itself under their nails

look
they always say with contagious glee
look what we've found

Zaffar Kunial

Tall Kahani

> *Straight answers were beyond the powers of Rashid Khalifa,*
> *who would never take a short cut if there was a longer, twistier*
> *road available.*
> Salman Rushdie, *Haroun and the Sea of Stories*

As bucket is to balti
so batty are the mad Bauls.
As quickly is to jaldi
a Qawwaal is a Sufi who calls.

As tale is to kahani
and lambi far too tall
so safar is our far journey
as sab is to everything. That's all.

But, Dad, *sab* is our word for partly or under.
And to *safar* is to be under strife.
And if *kaha* means 'where', and *nahii* means 'no',
then is *kahani* – your 'story' – from nowhere?

No, Son.
Only if your story is broken.
As zindagi is too

Dad – go on – don't break off.
What's *zindagi*? Or what's it like?
What's the story there?

That, my son, is just life.

Andrew McMillan

intimates

I'm wearing your underwear to the office
after a long fortnight of working
and not enough time to sort and wash
the stains that mark our progress through a day

I want to make a kink from this necessity
but don't get how   is it that undressing
later you'll see something of yourself
on me and want it back?   is it that I've taken

without asking   and this slight transgression
reframes me as a stranger?   is it
something about simply feeling closer?
the rub of the other against the self

in their absence?   I feel none of that
as I pull the boxers from a pile
where each identical pair smell of detergent
and are slightly too small for my body

which has spread   through comfort   since you moved in
but all day something of yours is hugging
close to the worst parts of myself   less than
a year a go   I could not have imagined
the possibility of something so wonderful

Andrew McNeillie

Homecoming

I came there, cap in hand,
as if a beggar to the day
or reverent soul before his maker.

I wish I could have stayed away
for the change I found there
and the change in me.

Faisal Mohyuddin

Partition, and Then

We were looking for _____ we found _____.
Carolyn Forché

The night is an empty basket, and the long journey ahead
promises to be weighed down by hunger, luminous

and wild. As they cross into the newly-formed nation,
a child, cargo strapped to her mother's back, takes the black

sheet of sky and folds it seven times to make a horse,
then fashions wings for it knitted from thin ribbons of wind.

Inside the brick temple of her mother's grasping heart,
a burning nest of nightjars, their feathers flecked with both

copper's shimmer and its blue decay. Their calls sound like stones
skipping across the surface of a river. Before the new day

tears open the stillness of her reveries, the girl rests her cheek
between her mother's shoulders and rolls herself back into

the womb. Inside, the rivers of the newly broken world
flow backwards toward the Himalayas, returning first to snow,

then to cloud. At the first blue blush of dawn, the child
begins to collect the stars, loses count, begins again, and then

again, until sleep arrives and she becomes a white ember of light,
exiled from her sky. In the distance, blindfolded theologians

straddle the gash drawn by Mountbatten's pen, holding vials
of new blood, large spoons carved from ivory, and honey.

Fiona Moore

Waking Up in a Basement

Even when I feel the stone weight of the house
and the earth of the hill it's built into
I don't really believe in my death—
not even when I sniff the draught that yesterday
was tainted by the smell of a small animal
decaying in the thistles and tangled grass
under the olive trees whose leaves fall
past the window like elegant rain.
This morning the smell isn't there.
At one time in the past I did, I think,
believe—I certainly lived day after day
in repeatedly unfolding horror.
The sun's come out sideways and is breaking up
orange across the folds of the duvet.
There's a blaze at the corner of my eye
that I need to not look at, partially veiled
though it is by these showers of leaves and
tree-trunks that knot and angle their way skywards.
The bell-tower strikes a half-hour.
The evidence of all the deaths it has tolled
is against me. The dead should crowd
my mind, as do the sweet chestnut and pine trees
that cloak this circular chain of hills.
A pair of shots ring out and the deep valley
moves the noise around: something, perhaps
a deer or wild boar or (heaven forfend) a
small bird may have died now, or be dying—
tasting its own blood amid a sense of
what panic or numb astonishment.

David Morley

The Grace of JCBs

Spring detonates on time thanks to wood anemones.
Woodland is wan without a million of them.

JCBs squat on fly-blown, gull-flocked hills.
They are King of Rat and glory to the gulls.

Wood anemones slink through crumbs of soil,
heads bowed by darkness, darkness limned by toil.

JCBs shovel rancid rubbish over tilth.
They rule by ramming everything in sight.

Anemones explode like stars or solar flare.
They glow and glister on the forest floor.

JCBs chew up tonnage and spit out filth.
Magpies choose their JCB and stick by *him*.

Wood anemones shift sidelong to the sun.
Their shoots are metronomes in slow emotion.

Rooks erupt in raptures around a JCB.
Their Midas, Grail, their Holy of Holies.

Wood anemones harvest ultraviolet rays.
Early bees are drawn droning to their gaze.

Nothing saddens a JCB more than a stalled JCB.
He ploughs across the planet to hold him, steady.

The lives of wood anemones are swift. We hail
their fleet and fleetness, their golden crisis.

JCBs squat on fly-blown, bird-flocked hills.
Spring detonates on time, thanks to JCBs.

Sean O'Brien

From the Cherry Hills

At dawn in this beautiful, bookish
Tree-lined town on the outskirts of Europe,

The air smells nimbly and sweetly of petrol
And the forest in its sunlit shroud

Of smoke and ideology reveals
That here among the Cherry Hills there lies

More history than any place can be
Imagined to accommodate, and so it burns.

Matter-of-fact as a date on a tomb,
Rebuilt from EU funds, the castle squats

On granite haunches by the slow Vrbas,
A place to keep the violence dry for now

While the chisels ring out where a single mosque
Of sixteen dynamited last time round

Is rising from its rubble to secure
A distant century against the infidel.

Smoke rises where the leaves are gathered.
More are falling. Let this warm November

Never end, and leave our group of skeletons
Companionably seated on the terrace

Beneath the black hoods of the folded umbrellas,
While the river below us flows on through itself

And away through the willows and out of sight
And we are still talking of poetry.

Conor O'Callaghan

Grace

They're coming to collect
the table I'm writing on.
They texted a while ago
to say they were leaving
a suburb four miles south.
Midweek, early evening:
traffic should be light.
I thought of sitting here
in gratitude, once more,
as long as supper lasts.
VINTAGE JOB LOT. My ad
hung weeks unanswered
in the whole foods co-op.
Then yesterday they called
to ask if I'd sell piecemeal.
Happily. The sun has drifted
slantwise of our building.
In the back lane behind me
two kitchen porters smoke
in what could be Cantonese.
For six years my things have
waited for the party I was
always threatening to throw.
There's the door...

                    They've been
and gone and bought the lot!
They were tremendously sweet:
she, Flemish, full of chat;
a fiancé with beard and bearing
of some prince in waiting.
They came for my table just
and took a shine to everything.

We laughed and lugged it all
to her employer's truck
parked running in the lane,
shook hands, wished luck
and hugged, for heaven's sake.
I came indoors to find
this notebook open on the floor
beneath my broken bread.
Thank you sideboard fetched
halfway across the Fens.
Thank you captain's chest,
handmade plywood bed,
mess benches from the war.
Thanks to all those friends
I shipped on for a song.
Thank you rooms in shade
that might yet prove to be
night already happening.
Thank you echoes echoing.
I have more hope in me
than I'd have ever guessed.

Ruth Padel

Set in Gold

This is death   late
        gentlest it could
              she was ninety-seven
                      shatterproof

her last word
        after *Where am I?*
             when we said we were all
                      all here with her

was   encouraging us   *Great*
    and Pluto took her
        lord of the underworld
           only god sworn to tell the truth.

Katherine Pierpoint

The egg-slicer

The kitchen drawer – the big, unloved one
you have to shove; the stoop-lowest to get at,
the one for the dishevelled, past-imperfect
with all its old fads, and its back-then must-haves –
I'm trawling through disorder for the egg-slicer
because things could do with cheering-up today
and I'm that kid   and I'm 55

Egg-slicer, thumb-strummer, joy-bringer –
O forget the eggs, the one thing is to *zing* it,
hamming it up on the egg-harp;
never enough of twangling near-Aeolian zithery tunes on it
up close to my ear, its tiny falsetto.
Little egg-lute, egg-mandolin,
spirited kitchen-kit, goblin wind –
even better than the piping-bag, with its screw-in nozzles
                                    and pibroch drone
of deftly-paced, worm-turn, squished-out flowers.

Egg-slicer, the grin-maker,
immediate music of the Clangers' spheres, cheesewires in space
and everything happy

****

Its day job was purposeful, and completely Yang
division. Forensic slices. Seventies salad.

All cool and white the bare egg would wait, unharrowed in its
plastic dimple, its hare's-form nest. Then
the wire portcullis would be drawn down; in small ceremony, and
always by a child. The scaled-down army bed-frame
in congress with the egg-moon, its ten rays
turned by Cardea, the both-ways, and linchpin,
                                    Goddess of the Hinge.

The egg would break one grey *Auspuffgas* of sulphur
and open outwards, through the wires; a lotus unfolded. Wafered,
it handed its white-gold coins to everyone.

But – just before that – as the pressure increases, and the egg will
            burst through its corsetry bustier,
the egg seemed to rise: to float, whole, through the wire –
like the ghost who walks unhurt through metal fences;
or campfire smoke, which sieves and riddles
                            through high twigs at night;
and how Lemmy's bass-strings were all tuned to X-sex, no matter
what the tight-rope note –
or what the pluck,
nor what wild metals
were spiking his head

Chris Preddle

On Mag Hill

1

I am self-absorbed, they tell me, unobservant
in worldly matters and obscurements, pernickety. Quite so.
But on Mag Hill like a dome or an observatory
one day in daylight I saw

Heaven: Dante's First Sphere, the Heaven of the Moon.
It turned slowly. Humans on it, or white semblances, could not be
    severed
from Absolute Love, it seemed. So many
had served like the blind poet and were saved.

We are sick for certitude. Perhaps
what I saw was a high may in may-time in hoop-
skirts of may. That slow medieval sky

misled us to wishfulness, to wistfulness for what's uncertain.
The Queen of the May of Mag Hill turned to me as a heaven turns.
Our certainty is of may-time, like hers.

2

Bending like Proserpina for weeds
of the middle summer, in these her usual gardening weeds

Jacqueline came and went, by the wood she lived under.
So the dead from their afterworld and underlife

came and went in time on Mag Hill,
themselves still, and out of time made equal.

One spoke to her. There is no perdition.
We see the amplitude of things with a last dispassionate

clearness, as you might in a fine
moral judgment, or the finest art. In fine,

there are absolutes to which you aspire
as Proserpina to the upper world. Say no prayers.

Speak to us while you have such substance. And Jacqueline would,
as she bent for the weeds closer to the wood.

3

They think I'm drier than cellophane,
the young who attend my course or cursus
on Heraclitus to Aquinas, metaphysics to form a self on,
a hope of unpassioned, or personed Final Causes;

but even I, on a walk like a long excursus
in a dry wood, I have seen the sylvan
Jacqueline gathering may-thorn, who discourses
with the white dead in wars or sickness fallen.

I think, therefore I feel. I feel, therefore I think
a woman in a wood
encloses the absolute. Whatever we think they're for,
thinkers, and things, are more than they are. The flesh is made
    word.
Jacqueline of the may, O I think her fair,
though I suffer dryness like a failed saint, or something untoward.

4

Jacqueline in may-time
would answer the dead who came to Mag Hill
as if to a hall of the dead. In my time

as in yours, we cannot make whole
the races we've made rackheaps of in Europe, or the waste
by her rivers of civilisation. Let newcomers come who will,

let us wear her new. We were never the wisest.
Absolutes we do not live with,
if they may be said to live. The west is what it was.

An absolute I cannot fall in love with,
for it contemplates itself in its own eternal summertime.
Lover, withe

the tangles of my may-time hair, for we have more time
than these unaltering dead, who were lovers sometime.

Meryl Pugh

Ugly Questions

Do you act like a hot girl or an ugly
girl? Do ugly girls ever get any boyfriends?
Do ugly people have any value? Should you
fuck ugly girls to improve your game? Should you
keep on being with an ugly girl
when there are no alternatives? Should you
hire ugly people? Are you hot, pretty,
average or ugly? Are ugly girls easy?
Are You Ugly, Cute, Hot, Or Head Turning
Sexy? (girls Only!!!) I am an ugly girl —
does that mean I will never get lucky? I
am an ugly woman. What chance do I have? Why are
the babies in medieval art so ugly?
Why are the emojis so ugly? Why are
the British so ugly? Why do engineers
use big old ugly computers? Why do foreigners
tend to marry women that are ugly?
Why do ugly boys get gorgeous girls?
If an ugly girl marries an ugly boy,
will the children too be ugly? If your child
were to be boring, stupid, or ugly, which one
would you prefer? Why didn't evolution
get rid of ugly people? Why are ugly
paintings so expensive? Why is LA
so ugly? Why is train seat fabric so ugly?
Why is gravel ugly? Why are models
ugly? Why are feet ugly? What is an ugly
stick? What are ugly tomatoes? What is ugly
crying? Is your current PowerPoint template
ugly? How do ugly people find love?

Denise Riley

Tick tock

A formal structure generates your thought.
Your mind will follow where the metre leads.
A poet hardly merits that 'well-wrought'
tick of approval from her critic, if he reads

her work for 'crafting' as its afterthought
to content; as if her lighter artifice needs
to trap in prosody what she'd first fought
to formulate in prose; as if a text proceeds

to turn 'poetic' a philosophy. Her retort:
that rhythm's own dictation soon exceeds
prior deliberation – cadence will thwart
prosaic forethought, as its ear lip-reads –

so 'sense must seem an echo to the sound'.
A natural music shapes this turnaround.

Antony Rowland

Newark

*I think the last pasty I bought was from the West
Cornwall Pasty Company.*
David Cameron

Chillax patsy with your fib pasty,
you try to buy kudos from a mind stall,
class largesse with the Beast of Bradford
on Newark North Gate seeking a Cornish:
do you flaunt your flaky walls on a pendolino,
gristle mince between your incisive incisors
in an onion-soaked delight, gravy gunged
beyond gelatine in a comfortable sack,
laugh at the possibility of stilton,
admire the chock of corner potato,
swerve a burn nibble devoid of filling,
pastry like a kiss without the squeeze
of lava cheddar or liver spills; or admit
to an order years too late? You are caught
in the floodlights of a forecourt, after
the pumps are hooked, plying a Ginster,
the flab of cellophane and its meat sludge.

Gorge instead on custards dipped in vanilla,
entreat your cousin Otter to express venison – which is,
    true to form, palpable beef
(not handsome, says Pepys) –
or binge on in-it-together jumbo sausage.
Learn from the Pasty Fest in Calumet,
Mexican paste in the state of Hidalgo,
Jamaican patties that shell the turnover,
Spanish empanadas quenched with fruit
and briks, pelmeni, ubiquitous samosas.
Or let there be, simply, some dainty Pork-Pye.

Take your spigarnel of spayne and break it
in a pot of good ale, where Eric his aching girth
would span/ And roar above his pasty pan.

Pudding Lane is burning down burning down burning down
The fleis und fisse pasty was refined in its fission
Quando fiam uti the cram of turnip? O swallow swallow
I sold my comforter to Billy Blake for a wortleberry pasty
These pasties I have shored against my ruins
Why then I'll brown you and your suet.
Flagons of hock and delicate ionckettes.

Pasty   pasty   pasty

Rachel Spence

Antonello's Song II (On a line by Dionne Brand)

I painted her in Venice,
        somewhere an absent light
warns of the rain to come
        and you can sleep with
a woman you'll never
        meet again yet step into
the vinegar plume
        of her scent hanging
in an alley hours after
        she has passed. Love
dried out by the monstrous
        wisdom of a city built
on water where pigments
        are sold in apothecaries'
shops and painting
        can heal you even as
the sky above the *calle*
        stretches to the Dolomites,
that mineral blue
        soaked out of lapis lazuli
from Persian caves,
        one mountain lending its language
to another, painful translations
        that leave you thirsty

Nic Stringer

from **Sisters**

For Hadewijch, Mechthild and Marguerite

i

The most important quality in a tapestry is beauty,
even if the picture is built from dark thoughts.
I have taken my belief further than is customary.

My first loom was a lap loom, using a simple edge.
A flat-woven gorgeous mess of finely coloured fibre;
cotton, worked with a gilt transverse thread.

No sound
No light
No weight in the air

Just a beater, passing between doubt and devotion;
objects and fears we choose to believe in – or not.
Faith, otherwise described.

ii

In the half-light, she sits at the loom
the process one of mediation
and negation. Like the warp threads
she is hidden in the completed work.
The allegory is of the Holy Wars
when the land overflowed
with empty women, not of home
or church – mystics and free spirits
to make the magisterium tremble
and shift their disappointed eyes.
Holding the yarn in high tension,

the men with the keys laughing
somewhere in the growing shadow
of Our Lady, her misgiving drags
on the narrow work, its truth spoiling
the buried silhouette of friends
and visionaries. She observes the biases.
The outline is certain but incomplete
like her, their favourite heretic
and solitary itinerant; beloved
as the mirror of simple souls.

Helen Tookey

On the Black Canal

Your boat is moored on the black canal
and the woman is playing the cello for you,

long low notes the colour of crows' wings.
You are a sound-box, air vibrates inside your bones

as each note elongates, a dark expanse –
are you under her protection, or is it a baffle

she draws around you, words becoming lost
in the rasp of bow against wire, your skull

full of overtones. Where were you trying to go that day
as you crossed the fields when the planes came,

droning low, forcing you down with the weight
of the sound in your head – you lay it seemed

for hours, pressed to the earth, unable to move
till the sound cleared, the weight eased

from your bones and you ran, away from
the terror of air, the fields' aphasic spaces.

Where were you going? You can't remember, and now
you're moored in the long box of your boat, and the woman

is playing the cello for you, the sound closing
over your head like black water, like crows' wings.

Ben Wilkinson

The Door

What was it that brought us out that day
from pints and talk, our corner snug,
down streets still slick with rain?

A mist had thickened to clinging fog –
the road deserted except distant traffic,
blinking away like lifeboats at sea.

Forgetting ourselves, it seemed a trick
when the city gave way to fields, empty
as all we weren't saying, but thinking.

I'm thinking now of that barn we saw.
Dilapidated, abandoned; sparrows darting
from its roof; but most of all the door

where no door was, bricked up
yet suddenly revealing itself,
like a portal between worlds.

Let's say it was. Let's say all we felt
stood there, all we've held off. Let's walk
through that door, love, and never look back.

Judith Willson

It's like the first winter morning

when you notice in the traffic
that tails down the valley, two – three –
bright cars with snow on their roofs

and you can't help looking up
to catch a rumour of pines and amber
and great bronze bells in a tower

above the two hundred steps of a citadel
where evening fall-winds stir sparks
out of dragon clawed braziers

and an owl's call carries the distance
from dark pooling under a forest
to first lilac light on the snowfields.

Sometimes we think this is how it could be.
How we think, sometimes, that it is.

James Womack

Oliver and the Bears

Empirically-minded little bastard,
he's stamping on the cracks between the stones.
A stamp, a pause, he looks around. 'No bears.
No bears, papa!' Of course there are no bears.
It's quiet today, the police have shotguns
as Oliver and I walk slowly to the market.
He's laughing: I don't really want to laugh;
he glances slanting and hangs from my arm.
I caught on TV this morning half a sentence
of unwitting metre, a lop-eared alexandrine:
We may not know exactly who we need to kill...
Now I think about it, a complete sentence:
it doesn't matter who was speaking.
Oliver wants to watch a street magician
hide himself in a box and disappear.
A good trick if you can sell it: mirrors?
Mass hypnosis? I'd like to know, today of all days.
'Come on now, Ol, there's no time, we're busy.'
There is time, but crowds make me uneasy.
A police car driven through the crowd,
clicking like a gunmetal dolphin.
Everything uncomfortable, the world
slightly at a slant to itself, balancing
on its own edge. You feel you need to be ready.
Oliver impatient now, pulls at my sleeve,
a pivot against the news dragging me outwards.
The necessary anchor. 'Papa, papa!'
He's pleased with himself; he's worked it all out.
'Papa, papa!' The self-belief of childhood,
unaware of the joy it inflicts on others.
'Papa, papa!' 'What is it?' 'Papa, no bears!'
I lie and say: 'You're right. No bears. No bears.'

November 2015. Europe

Andrew Wynn Owen

The Fountain

In dashing haste: the brilliancies of water
     Lap where the shorter
  Recessive rills are scattershot
     By silky light
That tumbles on, as evening turns to night
    Whether we look or not.

Carousing in the freefall of its shape,
     It circulates.
  Meanwhile, a vintner picks a grape
     And contemplates
The dogged revolution of the seasons,
    The roses and their reasons.

I rest in nature but the cause of nature
     Remains obscure:
  Equations and derivatives,
     A nomenclature
Of which I am, pursuing it, unsure.
    But thus the pattern lives.

It rambles through its indecisive ambit
     And I through mine,
  Our movements grounded in a gambit
     Of changing line,
So snatching ends that otherwise might scare
    By seeming not to care.

Its reeling carry-on is pseudorandom
     Yet, watched awhile,
  The liquid's helix falls in tandem
     With what I know
Of mind and matter. Yes, it's versatile.
   It's how our structures grow.

The sun beats down. Let's drop the psychopomp.
     It's just a splash
  Of water, a careening romp
     As fine as ash
Discarded on that muddle-king, the breeze.
   Now is your moment. Seize!

Biographies of the shortlisted writers

Forward Prize for Best Collection

Vahni Capildeo (b. 1973 Port of Spain, Trinidad and Tobago) won the Forward Prize for Best Collection in 2016 with *Measures of Expatriation*. Asked about future projects in a subsequent interview, Capildeo spoke of writing 'thing-like poems which did not belong in any of the recent books: moss, glass, lizard words'. Some of these have found their way into *Venus as a Bear*, a collection that explores the strange affinities humans have for creatures, objects and places.

Capildeo's poetry deliberately resists purely biographical interpretation: the author elects to be identified as 'they/them' in the context of their work. They came to the UK in 1991 to study English and then Old Norse at Christ Church, Oxford, and to work for the *Oxford English Dictionary*. Their advice for anyone starting out in poetry today is simple: 'Delete Facebook. Go outdoors.'

Toby Martinez de las Rivas (b. 1978 Winchester) moved from north-east England to Córdoba after the publication of his first collection, *Terror*, in 2014. In an interview with Lucy Mercer he described how the 'black sun' of his new collection's title developed from the small black circles which served as *Terror*'s section dividers. 'Some time after *Terror* went to press I was toying around with images and motifs. I sketched a much larger circle into a document and infilled it with black, and I was suddenly aware of it as a presence separate from me... I found something terrible about it, about its featureless, even, dense nothingness. But I sensed some kind of glory in it, too.'

The poems of *Black Sun* take their place on that line between terror and glory which characterises the best religious poetry. Asked what advice he would give to his younger self, he writes: 'Be cautious. Not too cautious. Believe in language.'

JO Morgan (b. 1978 Edinburgh) is the son of a former RAF officer, who was involved in maintaining Britain's Airborne Nuclear Deterrent. *Assurances* is Morgan's response to his father's tremendous responsibility: it eavesdrops on the thoughts of those trying to understand and justify their roles in keeping peace by threatening war. Those overheard include civilians unaware of danger, enemy agents, the whirring machines and even the bomb itself.

Morgan, who lives on a farm in the Scottish Borders, is the author of five previous collections, each, like *Assurances*, a single book-length poem. *Natural Mechanical* won the Aldeburgh First Collection Prize, and was shortlisted for the Felix Dennis Prize for Best First Collection; *Interference Pattern*, the first of his collections to be published by Cape, was shortlisted for the TS Eliot Prize.

Danez Smith (b. 1989 Minnesota, USA) writes poems which are simultaneously jubilant and confrontational. Their debut, *[insert] boy*, won the Lambda Literary Award and the Kate Tufts Discovery Award. After their poem 'dear white america' – included in *Don't Call Us Dead* – was featured on PBS NewsHour, Smith's performance received 300,000 YouTube views in the space of a few days.

Smith is African-American, queer, gender-neutral and HIV positive. They first became aware of the possibilities of contemporary poetry through HBO's *Def Poetry*, and honed their performance skills with theatre training and slams (Smith is the reigning Rustbelt Individual Champion). The poems which excite them most, they say, are those which 'through language, better equip me to re-enter the world and proceed vigorously'.

Tracy K Smith (b. 1972 Massachusetts, USA) is the poet laureate of the United States. She began writing poems aged 10, but it was not until she lost her mother to cancer at 22 that poetry became, in her words, 'a tool for living'.

The four books she published prior to *Wade in the Water* established her as one of the most exciting poets in the USA. In 2012 she won the Pulitzer Prize for *Life on Mars* – a collection she has described as 'looking out to the universe and forward to an imagined future'; *Wade in the Water*, by contrast, looks 'earthward and backward', confronting unflinchingly the moral crises of race and history in America.

Smith is also a librettist and translator. She is currently writing the libretto for an opera entitled *Castor and Patience*, and co-translating the work of the contemporary Chinese poet Yi Lei.

Felix Dennis Prize for Best First Collection

Kaveh Akbar (b. 1989 Tehran, Iran) teaches at Purdue University, Indiana, and is the founding editor of *Divedapper*, a journal devoted to interviews with poets. His first published poem, aged seven, was called 'A Packer Poem', and took as its subject matter the Green Bay Packers football team. *Calling a Wolf a Wolf* has darker concerns at its heart: alcoholism, desire, faith. He has described it as an unconventional addiction recovery narrative, 'less focused on war stories and more on the psycho/physio/cosmological implications of addiction and recovery'.

As a very young child in Tehran, Akbar was taught by his parents to pray in Arabic, a language none of them spoke. This idea of a special, secret language would become the bedrock for his conception of poetry: 'the understanding that language has a capacity beyond the mere relay of semantic data, that if a line could be spoken with sufficient beauty and conviction, it might thin the membrane between its speaker and whichever divine (God, desire, despair, the mind, the body) they wish to address'.

Abigail Parry (b. 1983 UK) worked as a toymaker for seven years, and the poems in *Jinx* bear a resemblance to dangerous toys or games: patterned surfaces, concealments, trick doors, and sliding panels abound. She began thinking seriously about how poems worked when she read Maura Dooley's 'History' for the first time: 'It fascinated me: you could take it apart, like an engine, and examine every part to see what it was doing; at the same time, it worked a spell, and you can't see the joins in a spell.'

She used money earned while travelling with a circus to join Maura Dooley's creative writing MA course at Goldsmith's in 2008. Parry published her first poems under pseudonyms: 'I wanted to have the option of jettisoning this or that identity if it didn't work out.' In 2016, she won the Ballymaloe International Poetry Prize, the Free Verse Poetry Book Fair Competition and the International Troubadour Prize.

Phoebe Power (b. 1992 Newcastle-upon-Tyne) was a Foyle Young Poet of the year before studying at Cambridge, where she ran the Pembroke Poetry Society. Her pamphlet *Harp Duet* was published by Eyewear Publishing. The poems in *Shrines of Upper Austria* take their bearings from the landscapes and local detail of Austria, sometimes incorporating and assimilating whole lines of German among the English. Several of the poems draw from the life-story of her Austrian grandmother, Christl.

Power says that, 'You can never be sure how readers will engage with your work when you write it – readers are all different – so knowing that some people have connected with it is truly a joy.' Her enthusiasm for different modes of engagement has included adapting her poems into collaborative video installations and performance pieces, featuring harps, electronica and a flood-destroyed piano.

Shivanee Ramlochan (b. 1986 St. Joseph, Trinidad and Tobago) works as an arts journalist and blogger in Trinidad. The daughter of a teacher, she grew up surrounded by books. She says that 'poetry was part of my earliest experiences in reading, so that I remember books that were not poems as though they were'.

Poetry for Ramlochan is a work of witness: the central thread of *Everyone Knows I Am a Haunting*, 'The Red Thread Cycle', addresses and gives voice to survivors of sexual assault. 'Some of the poems are as they emerged, almost as if gifted, with me as a startled conduit of interpretation', she says. 'Others have been worked and reworked, finessed, hewn and shattered and restitched, to say what they must.' The idea of a poem which says what it must – which speaks with its own unmistakable interior voice, and leaves the poet 'awestruck and bewildered' – is central to Ramlochan's practice as a writer.

Richard Scott (b. 1981 London) used to be an opera singer but the 'inhuman rigours' of the profession left him seeking escape. 'After years of obsessing over texts, librettos and poetry that had been set to music, poetry seemed to me like almost a logical step. It became clear to me that when you took the music away, there was still a "music" and a rhythm to the poem – and that fascinated me.'

His chapbook *Wound* won the 2016 Michael Marks Award. The following year, he won the *Poetry London* competition with 'crocodile', a poem at the centre of many of the trajectories in *Soho* – submergence, flesh, the vulnerability of queer bodies. Its snapping linebreaks and sharp images remind the reader that he is, above all else, a thrilling poet.

Forward Prize for Best Single Poem

Fiona Benson (b. 1978 Wiltshire) began keeping a special notebook for poetry, as distinct from song lyrics, at the age of 17. A Faber New Poet, her first collection, *Bright Travellers*, won the Seamus Heaney Prize. A second collection, *Vertigo & Ghost*, from which her shortlisted poem is taken, is forthcoming from Cape Poetry in 2019.

Benson describes 'Ruins' as 'a poem that tries to look at a real, hardworking, postnatal, middle-aged body. I like that while it starts with dismay, it pivots on the recognition of the lopsided stomach into a celebration of what the body housed.' She welcomes the new awareness and openness she discerns towards these themes in contemporary poetry. She describes the Forward shortlisting as 'a validation of poems that write of the body, of the domestic realm, and of familial love, (it) says "yes, these subjects are of interest, they really matter"… and I agree. They do'.

Liz Berry (b. 1980 Black Country) was selected for the Jerwood/Arvon mentoring scheme in 2011. With the encouragement of her mentor Daljit Nagra she incorporated the Black Country dialect of her childhood into her poetry. The resulting collection, *Black Country*, won the Felix Dennis Prize for Best First Collection.

Berry's 'The Republic of Motherhood' is the title poem of a forthcoming pamphlet, describing the experience of becoming a new mother. The poem responds both to the support she received from other mothers after the birth of her first son, and to a literary absence. 'Our stories were beautiful, raw, heartbroken, joyous and deep beyond reckoning. But when I looked to poems, the places that had always comforted me, that experience was hard to find.' In 'The Republic of Motherhood', Berry extends her project of drawing comfort from the hard-to-reckon-with.

Sumita Chakraborty (b. 1987 New York, USA) was awarded the Ruth Lilly and Dorothy Sargent Rosenberg Poetry Fellowship from the Poetry Foundation in 2017. She describes her ideal poem as one that 'will write into being a world that already in some way exists'.

Her shortlisted poem, 'And death demands a labor', takes its title from a line of Rilke's. She has described it as an 'imagined elegy' for her father. 'After having hassled at it unsuccessfully for years,' she says, 'one evening I walked back into my apartment after a full and ordinary day, sat down on my bed and rewrote it in a single go.'

Chakraborty has recently completed both the manuscript of her first full collection, *O Spirit*, and her PhD thesis for Emory University, Georgia.

Jorie Graham (b. 1950 New York, USA) was expelled from the Sorbonne for participating in the 1968 student protests. She has since published 14 collections of poems, most recently *Fast*. Over the years she has won the Pulitzer Prize, the Wallace Stevens Award, the Nonino Prize and, in 2012, the Forward Prize for Best Collection. She teaches at Harvard.

The crown of branches which Graham conjures in her shortlisted poem 'Tree' – 'full of secrecy insight immensity vigour bursting complexity' – might also describe her own poetic. Her characteristic long lines and jolts of syntax illuminate the held objects suddenly and very brightly. 'Tree' shows us, too, the process of its own making: 'The imagination tried to go here when we asked it to, from where I hold the / fruit in my right hand, but it would not go.'

Will Harris (b. 1989 London) is the author of *Mixed-Race Superman* – an essay examining resilience and self-creation, which takes as subjects Keanu Reeves, Barack Obama and Harris's own Anglo-Indonesian heritage – as well as a chapbook, *All This is Implied*, winner of the LRB Bookshop Poetry Pick for best pamphlet. A selection of his work was included in *Ten: Poems of the New Generation*; a full collection, provisionally entitled *Rendang*, is currently in the works.

Harris began his shortlisted poem, 'SAY', after his father fell ill. He describes it as being 'about my dad's breached body; about fear and borders; about our desire for wholeness and purity; and about the illusion of flow that can only be maintained by violence'. It was drafted in flight, on the back of a Ryanair boarding pass.

Publisher acknowledgements

Kaveh Akbar · Yeki Blood Yeki Nabood · Neither Now Nor Never ·
  Calling a Wolf a Wolf · Penguin Books
Hera Lindsay Bird · Monica · *Hera Lindsay Bird* · Penguin Books
Fiona Benson · Ruins · *Wild Court*
Liz Berry · The Republic of Motherhood · *Granta*
Sean Borodale · Eastwater Cavern Voice-Test · *Asylum* · Cape Poetry
Graham Burchell · Resurrection · Bridport Prize
Marianne Burton · For A Long Time He Was Very Childish ·
  Kierkegaard's Cupboard · Seren
Toby Campion · When the Stranger Called Me a Faggot ·
  Through your blood · Burning Eye Books
Vahni Capildeo · Day, with Hawk · Bullshit · *Venus as a Bear* · Carcanet
JP Carpenter · *from* Notes on the Voyage of Owl and Girl · *An Ocean of
Static* · Penned in the Margins
Sumita Chakraborty · And death demands a labor · *PN Review*
Sophie Collins · Healers · *Who Is Mary Sue?* · Faber & Faber
Sarah Corbett · The Unicorn · *A Perfect Mirror* · Pavilion Poetry
Emily Critchley · Something wonderful was happened it is called you ·
  Ten Thousand Things · Boiler House Press
Paul Deaton · That Bang · *A Watchful Astronomy* · Seren
Christopher Deweese · I was a wartime censor · *The Confessions* ·
  Periplum Poetry
Imtiaz Dharker · Wolf, Words · *Luck is the Hook* · Bloodaxe Books
Tishani Doshi · Girls Are Coming Out of the Woods ·
  Girls Are Coming Out of the Woods · Bloodaxe Books
Sarah Doyle · The woman who married an alchemist · *The Fenland Reed*
Sasha Dugdale · For Edward Thomas · *Joy* · Carcanet
Kate Edwards · Frequency Violet · *Ink Sweat & Tears*
Richard Georges · Now / Tortola · *Giant* · Platypus Press
Jorie Graham · Tree · *London Review of Books*
Lucy Hamilton · Blood Letting · *Of Hearts & Heads* · Shearsman Books
Philip Hancock · The Girl from the Triangle House · *City Works Dept.* ·
  CB Editions
Will Harris · SAY · *The Poetry Review*

Winners of the Forward Prizes

Best Collection

2017 · Sinéad Morrissey · *On Balance* · Carcanet

2016 · Vahni Capildeo · *Measures of Expatriation* · Carcanet

2015 · Claudia Rankine · *Citizen: An American Lyric* · Penguin Books

2014 · Kei Miller · *The Cartographer Tries to Map a Way to Zion* · Carcanet

2013 · Michael Symmons Roberts · *Drysalter* · Cape Poetry

2012 · Jorie Graham · *PLACE* · Carcanet

2011 · John Burnside · *Black Cat Bone* · Cape Poetry

2010 · Seamus Heaney · *Human Chain* · Faber & Faber

2009 · Don Paterson · *Rain* · Faber & Faber

2008 · Mick Imlah · *The Lost Leader* · Faber & Faber

2007 · Sean O'Brien · *The Drowned Book* · Picador Poetry

2006 · Robin Robertson · *Swithering* · Picador Poetry

2005 · David Harsent · *Legion* · Faber & Faber

2004 · Kathleen Jamie · *The Tree House* · Picador Poetry

2003 · Ciaran Carson · *Breaking News* · The Gallery Press

2002 · Peter Porter · *Max is Missing* · Picador Poetry

2001 · Sean O'Brien · *Downriver* · Picador Poetry

2000 · Michael Donaghy · *Conjure* · Picador Poetry

1999 · Jo Shapcott · *My Life Asleep* · OUP

1998 · Ted Hughes · *Birthday Letters* · Faber & Faber

1997 · Jamie McKendrick · *The Marble Fly* · OUP

1996 · John Fuller · *Stones and Fires* · Chatto & Windus

1995 · Sean O'Brien · *Ghost Train* · OUP

1994 · Alan Jenkins · *Harm* · Chatto & Windus

1993 · Carol Ann Duffy · *Mean Time* · Anvil Press

1992 · Thom Gunn · *The Man with Night Sweats* · Faber & Faber

Best First Collection

2017 · Ocean Vuong · *Night Sky with Exit Wounds* · Cape Poetry

2016 · Tiphanie Yanique · *Wife* · Peepal Tree

2015 · Mona Arshi · *Small Hands* · Pavilion Poetry

2014 · Liz Berry · *Black Country* · Chatto & Windus

2013 · Emily Berry · *Dear Boy* · Faber & Faber

2012 · Sam Riviere · *81 Austerities* · Faber & Faber

2011 · Rachael Boast · *Sidereal* · Picador Poetry

2010 · Hilary Menos · *Berg* · Seren

2009 · Emma Jones · *The Striped World* · Faber & Faber

2008 · Kathryn Simmonds · *Sunday at the Skin Launderette* · Seren

2007 · Daljit Nagra · *Look We Have Coming to Dover!* · Faber & Faber

2006 · Tishani Doshi · *Countries of the Body* · Aark Arts

2005 · Helen Farish · *Intimates* · Cape Poetry

2004 · Leontia Flynn · *These Days* · Cape Poetry

2003 · AB Jackson · *Fire Stations* · Anvil Press

2002 · Tom French · *Touching the Bones* · The Gallery Press

2001 · John Stammers · *Panoramic Lounge-Bar* · Picador Poetry

2000 · Andrew Waterhouse · *In* · The Rialto

1999 · Nick Drake · *The Man in the White Suit* · Bloodaxe Books

1998 · Paul Farley · *The Boy from the Chemist is Here to See You* · Picador Poetry

1997 · Robin Robertson · *A Painted Field* · Picador Poetry

1996 · Kate Clanchy · *Slattern* · Chatto & Windus

1995 · Jane Duran · *Breathe Now, Breathe* · Enitharmon

1994 · Kwame Dawes · *Progeny of Air* · Peepal Tree

1993 · Don Paterson · *Nil Nil* · Faber & Faber

1992 · Simon Armitage · *Kid* · Faber & Faber

Best Single Poem

2017 · Ian Patterson · The Plenty of Nothing · *PN Review*

2016 · Sasha Dugdale · Joy · *PN Review*

2015 · Claire Harman · The Mighty Hudson · *Times Literary Supplement*

2014 · Stephen Santus · In a Restaurant · Bridport Prize

2013 · Nick MacKinnon · The Metric System · *The Warwick Review*

2012 · Denise Riley · A Part Song · *London Review of Books*

2011 · RF Langley · To a Nightingale · *London Review of Books*

2010 · Julia Copus · An Easy Passage · *Magma*

2009 · Robin Robertson · At Roane Head · *London Review of Books*

2008 · Don Paterson · Love Poem for Natalie "Tusja" Beridze · *The Poetry Review*

2007 · Alice Oswald · Dunt · *Poetry London*

2006 · Sean O'Brien · Fantasia on a Theme of James Wright · *The Poetry Review*

2005 · Paul Farley · Liverpool Disappears for a Billionth of a Second · *The North*

2004 · Daljit Nagra · Look We Have Coming to Dover! · *The Poetry Review*

2003 · Robert Minhinnick · The Fox in the Museum of Wales · *Poetry London*

2002 · Medbh McGuckian · She Is in the Past, She Has This Grace · *The Shop*

2001 · Ian Duhig · The Lammas Hireling · National Poetry Competition

2000 · Tessa Biddington · The Death of Descartes · Bridport Prize

1999 · Robert Minhinnick · Twenty-five Laments for Iraq · *PN Review*

1998 · Sheenagh Pugh · Envying Owen Beattie · *New Welsh Review*

1997 · Lavinia Greenlaw · A World Where News Travelled Slowly · *Times Literary Supplement*

1996 · Kathleen Jamie · The Graduates · *Times Literary Supplement*

1995 · Jenny Joseph · In Honour of Love · *The Rialto*

1994 · Iain Crichton Smith · Autumn · *PN Review*

1993 · Vicki Feaver · Judith · *Independent on Sunday*

1992 · Jackie Kay · Black Bottom · Bloodaxe Books

For more detail and further reading about the Forward Prizes, books and associated programmes, see our website forwardartsfoundation.org or follow us on Facebook or Twitter @ForwardPrizes

Supporting Poetry Through This Book

Proceeds from the sale of this book go towards the Forward Arts
Foundation, which promotes public knowledge, understanding and
enjoyment of poetry in the UK and Ireland. We are a charity committed
to widening poetry's audience, honouring achievement and supporting
talent: our programmes include National Poetry Day and the Forward
Prizes for Poetry. Through our projects we work with schools, libraries,
publishers and members of the public across the British Isles.